BACHELOR UNDONE

BACHELOR UNDONE

Brenda Jackson

CHIVERS

British Library Cataloguing in Publication Data available

This Large Print edition published by AudioGO Ltd, Bath, 2013.
Published by arrangement with Harlequin Enterprises II B.V./S à r.l.

U.K. Hardcover   ISBN   978 1 4713 1983 9
U.K. Softcover   ISBN   978 1 4713 1984 6

Printed and bound in Great Britain by
TJ International Limited

Dear Reader,

Please envision six men who, for various reasons, are members of the Bachelor in Demand Club, and are determined to stay single for as long as they can. With each book I write in this series, I am having fun making each man open their hearts to love when the right woman comes along.

Bachelor Undone is York Ellis's story, and his leading lady is Darcy Owens. Both York and Darcy are strong-willed individuals who think they know what they want, and who stubbornly refuse to admit their true heart's desire is to want each other. York has his own agenda and Darcy has hers, but they soon discover that what the mind sometimes refuses to accept, the heart ultimately will.

I hope all of you enjoy reading York and Darcy's story.

Happy reading!

Brenda Jackson

To the love of my life,
Gerald Jackson, Sr.

To all the family, friends
and dedicated readers.
This one is for you.

For God hath not given us the spirit of fear; but of power, and of love, and of a sound mind.

— II *Timothy* 1:7

PROLOGUE

Spending her vacation in New York during the month of December was not on Darcelle Owens's list of things to do, which was why she was in a cab headed for JFK International Airport. She loved living in the Big Apple, but when forecasters had predicted the city's coldest winter ever, she was glad she had plans to get the hell out of Dodge.

Jamaica, here I come, she thought relaxing back in her seat. While her coworkers would be battling the snow, she planned to be lying half-naked on the beach under the heat of the Jamaican sun. And then at night, she'd become a sophisticated hooch and let her hair down, party and even do a little man-hunting. She deserved it after working her tail off the past two years.

She had the whole month of December off and would have loved to spend the entire time in Jamaica. But her parents expected her to come home for Christmas, as usual. She got a chill in her bones just thinking of returning to Minneapolis for even a little while.

She'd always hated cold weather and would have headed south to attend college if her parents hadn't convinced her of how much money they could save not having to pay out-of-state tuition. When she talked to her mother just that morning, it was twenty below zero. *Brrrr.*

And then her best friend Ellie Lassiter expected her to spend a few days with her at her lake house in North Carolina before Ellie and her husband Uriel's New Year's Eve bash.

Darcy planned to keep her family and Ellie happy, but first she intended to relax in the warm weather for at least three weeks.

Darcy cringed when she heard the chime of a text message on her cell phone. How dare her younger brother Prescott teach their mother how to text! Darcy bet between her, Prescott and her older brother Jonas that their mother, Joan Owens, sent out over one hundred text messages a day. Okay, maybe she was exaggerating a tad bit, but it would seem about that number.

Checking her phone, Darcy smiled when she saw the message hadn't come from her mother after all. It was from Ellie.

Behave yourself in J. Have fun. E

Darcy chuckled and quickly texted back. Can't behave myself and have fun, too. LOL.

Got Bruce with you? the responding text asked.

Darcy's smile widened. Bruce was the name she'd given her little sex toy. Nope. Left Bruce behind this time. I hope to get lucky and find someone who's looking to have some fun. Looking forward to relaxing, reading and replacing Bruce with the real thing.

She wasn't surprised when within seconds of sending that message her cell phone rang. Of course it was Ellie. "Yes, El?"

"And just what do you mean by that?" her best friend asked.

Darcy threw her head back and laughed. "Just what I said. It's time Bruce goes into retirement. He's earned it."

"Girl, you're awful."

"No, I'm not. If I was awful, I wouldn't have gone without being in a relationship for two years. If it hadn't been for Bruce and my romance novels, I don't know what I would have done to keep sane."

And that was so true. She had moved from Minneapolis after taking a job as a city plan- ner for New York City. Over the past two years, she had been working day and night trying to prove the city hadn't made a mistake by hiring an outsider.

She had worked hard and hadn't taken any time off other than the recognized holidays, which was why she had accumulated so much vacation time. And now she intended to enjoy it. It was the end of the year, and her boss had warned her to "use it or lose it." The only thing she planned to lose was two years of abstinence.

"Chill, El," she said when there was silence on the other end. "I'm taking plenty of condoms with me if that makes you happy."

She glanced up and saw the elderly cab-driver looking at her looking in the rearview mirror. *Oops.* She couldn't do anything but smile. She lowered her head and whispered into the phone. "Look, you're going to get me in trouble, El. The cabbie heard my remark about condoms and is looking at me funny. Like he thinks I'm a loose woman or something."

"Nobody's fault but your own for saying what you did."

"It's the truth."

"Whatever. Go and have your fun, but be careful, stay safe and you better have a lot to tell me when you get back."

Darcy felt giddy all the way to her toes.

"Trust me, I will. I intend to become one of the heroines in those romance novels I enjoy reading so much. And I got this hot pink bikini with the word *seduction* written all over it."

Darcy then clicked off the phone and glanced out the cab's window. It had started snowing. She drew in a deep breath thinking she couldn't get to Jamaica fast enough.

York Ellis, former NYPD officer and present-day security expert, felt adrenaline flow through his veins. It was always that way at the start of a new case, and from the sound of things, this one would be a challenge. As far as he was concerned, anything would top the last case he had protecting the horse who'd won the Kentucky Derby when rumors of a horse-napping had begun circulating.

He glanced across his desk at Malcolm Overstreet, renowned director and screenwriter. Malcolm was there to represent a group of New York filmmakers whose movies were getting put on the black market before they got the chance to be released to theaters. This was causing the filmmakers enormous loss of profits and almost forcing them into bankruptcy. In this case, the actual movie footage was being sold while the production was still in process. Certain scenes were even appearing on the internet.

On top of that, idle threats had been made against the making of a controversial movie. Malcolm wanted York's firm to find out who was behind the bootlegging as well as handle the security for the movie.

York had enough people working for him to do the latter, and as far as finding out who was involved in advance footage being released to the public, he figured with the right plan in place that should be easy enough.

"Have you ever considered the possibility this might be an inside job?" he asked Malcolm. He could tell from the man's expression that he hadn't.

"We have good people working for our production company," Malcolm said. "If we lose money, they lose money."

Not necessarily, York thought. "When does the movie continue shooting?" he asked.

"Next week in Jamaica," Malcolm responded.

York nodded as he jotted down a few notes. He knew the film was a controversial biography on the life of Marcus Garvey, the black civil rights activist from Jamaica. And he knew it would depict a side of Garvey that some didn't want told — which was the reason for the heightened security while they were on the island. "Has any current cast or crew member worked on your last couple of movies?"

"Yes, we usually hire the same crew for all our productions. Some of them have been with us for years, and it's hard to imagine them being a part of anything illegal."

"What about your cast?"

"Johnny Rush is my leading man as Garvey, and Danielle Simone is my leading lady as his love interest. But you can scratch them off the list," Malcolm said confidently.

York lifted a brow. "Why are you so sure?"

"Their egos. Both are too vain to want their work anywhere other than the big screen, trust me. They think having their work out on the black market is an insult to their talent. In fact, the only way they would agree to work with Spirit Head Productions again is if we assured them their work will not be undermined and hit the streets before a premier date."

"What about Damien Felder?" York asked, glancing down at the papers on his desk. "I've noticed his name has shown up on probably every production you've done."

Malcolm nodded. "You can mark Damien's name off the list as well. He's my line producer, and a cut in our profits slashes into his bank account as well. He has nothing to gain from our movies appearing on the black market. If another one of our movies gets bootlegged, we'll be filing for bankruptcy."

Malcolm then leaned forward. "I believe whoever is behind things will try and get the footage sometime while my cast and crew are shooting the final scenes in Jamaica. And I want you to make sure that doesn't happen, York. My partners and I are sick and tired of losing money that way. It's not fair not only to us but to every person who has a stake in the production."

The man paused and then added, "And then there's this threat on Rush. Some think he fabricated things for publicity, but we can't take any chances."

York closed his notepad. Malcolm and his group were heavy hitters who could open the doors to even more business for York's security firm. But more importantly, it was the principle of the thing. Someone was breaking the law and cutting into the profits — actually outright stealing them — and they were profits they didn't deserve.

He knew one of the main reasons Malcolm had come to him was because Malcolm was a friend of his father's. Malcolm had also attended Morehouse College as a young man along with York's father and five godfathers before getting a graduate degree from Columbia University Film School. "I understand, and I intend to fly to Jamaica immediately and find out who is behind things."

Malcolm lifted a brow. "Will it be that easy?"

York met the man's gaze with an intense look. "No, but once I establish my cover, I'll be a regular on set and I can keep an eye on what's going on. And the six men and three women working for me are the best of the best. Rest assured, whoever is behind this has messed with one of your productions for the last time."

CHAPTER 1

Darcy stood on the balcony and glanced out at the beach. It was hard to believe this was her third day in Jamaica and she was just getting out of her hotel room today for the first time. She, who rarely got sick, had gotten a stomach virus her first day and had stayed in her hotel room in bed. What a bummer of a way to start off her vacation.

The good thing was that today she was feeling like her old self again, and she intended to spend as much time outside as she possibly could. She had lost two valuable days, but from here on out it was full steam ahead.

When she had checked in, the hotel clerk had given her a list of the hotel's activities for the week, and tonight they would be hosting a classy beach party. Her health had improved just in time. A party was the last thing she wanted to miss.

She turned away from the window and

crossed the room to glance at herself in the full-length mirror. She had purchased the wide-brimmed straw hat from a gift shop at the airport, and the sundress she was wearing had caught her eye the moment she'd seen it at Macy's over the summer. At the time, a trip to Jamaica had been just a fancy, and in a way, it was hard to believe she was actually here.

Instead of donning a bikini and lying on the beach today, she thought she would take a tour of the island and get some sightseeing in. She had purchased a new digital camera and intended to put it to good use. And she definitely intended to do some shopping. When she had visited Jamaica a few years ago — a college graduation present from her parents — she had purchased several pieces of jewelry that had been handcrafted by an island woman. Darcy intended to see if the small shop near the pier was still there. There were several more pieces she would love to add to her collection.

She glanced around the room. Since she would be here for three weeks she'd decided to get one of the residential suites, and she loved it. It was huge and spacious, and although it was costing her a pretty penny, it was worth it. Besides, she deserved it.

The furniture in the sitting area was

elegant and the decor colors of cream, yellow, mint green and plum perfectly reflected an island theme. Floor-to-ceiling windows lined one wall and provided a balcony view of the water.

French doors led from the sitting room directly into the bedroom, which had its own balcony. There was nothing like waking up to the beauty of the Caribbean Sea. But it was the bathroom that she'd found simply breathtaking. It had a dressing room area and a closet large enough to camp out in if the need arose. Then there was the humongous Jacuzzi tub that could hold several couples if you were inclined to get that kinky . . . which she wasn't. She wasn't into sharing of any kind when it came to relationships.

Grabbing her purse off the table, she headed for the door. It was a beautiful day, and she planned to spend as much of it as she could outside. Then she would return and take a shower and a nap before getting ready for the party tonight.

York walked along the pier. It hadn't taken any time to get his game plan in place and head toward the island. Jamaica was beautiful, but unlike all the other times he came to the island, he was here for business.

Regardless of what Malcolm thought, every member of the cast and crew was a suspect. His team had divided the list, and every single person was being checked out. He was hoping it wouldn't take long to expose the culprit since he planned to spend the holidays back in the States. His parents had moved to Seattle a few years ago and luckily didn't expect everyone to show up on their doorsteps for the holidays. In fact, as long as he could remember, once he and his siblings began having lives of their own, his parents would spend the holidays in Toronto, visiting friends they had there. Usually York would spend a quiet Christmas at home, and those times he wanted company, he had five sets of godparents he could visit.

Most people knew the story as to how six guys who'd met and become best friends while attending Morehouse had on graduation day made a pact to stay in touch by becoming godfathers to each of their children and that the firstborn sons' names would carry the letters of the alphabet from *U* to *Z*. And that was how Uriel Lassiter, Virgil Bougard, Winston Coltrane, Xavier Kane, York Ellis and Zion Blackstone had come into existence. He was close to his godparents and godbrothers and couldn't imagine them not being a part of his life.

He checked his watch. A couple of his men had checked in already with their reports, and it was obvious Malcolm didn't know some of his people as well as he thought he did. However, there was nothing to indicate any of them could be suspected of anything other than engaging in a number of illicit affairs.

York glanced around and saw he was the object of several women's attention. He didn't mind, and if he'd had the time, he would even indulge their fantasies. He was well aware that a number of women came to the island alone to get their groove on. They were manhunters who were only looking for a good time.

He kept walking. He was on assignment, and there wasn't a woman he'd met yet who could make him take his mind off work.

Darcy squinted against the brightness of the sun while moving from shop to shop in Montego Bay. Reggae music seemed to be playing just about everywhere. Pausing, she pulled out her sunglasses to shield her eyes from the sun. It was hard to believe how bright it shone here when, according to weather reports, it was still snowing in New York.

She stopped at a fruit stand, admiring the basket of strawberries, all plump and ripe, when something out of the corner of her eye caught her attention.

A man.

And boy, what a man he was. She could only see his profile, but even from almost fifteen feet away she could tell he was a fine specimen of the opposite sex. He was in a squatting position, going through a rack of T-shirts that some peddler was trying to sell him.

Darcy tilted the sunglasses a little off her eyes to get a better view, deciding she didn't want to miss anything — especially the way the denim of his jeans managed to stretch tight across his thighs. And the way his shoulders filled the shirt he was wearing.

He stood up a little and his tush — OMG, it was definitely the kind a woman would drool over. She bet they were perfect masculine cheeks, firm and fine.

Her mind began working, and she immediately began seeing him as a hero from one of the romance novels she read. *But which one?* she asked herself, thumping her finger against her chin.

She immediately thought of Jansen Trumble, the bad boy from the spicy novel *Mine Until Morning.* That had been one hot book, and even after reading it at least four or five times, she would give just about anything to have a rumble with Trumble. She settled her sunglasses back on her eyes thinking if she couldn't have the fictional Trumble then a look-alike would have to suffice.

"Miss, would you like to try some of my strawberries? I just rinsed this batch off. I bet you'd like them."

Her attention was pulled momentarily away from the gorgeous hunk when an island woman offered her a tray of fresh strawberries, sill wet from a recent rinsing. "Thanks, I'd love to try one."

She popped a strawberry in her mouth, immediately enjoying the taste when the sweet flavor burst on her tongue. It was wet, juicy and so delicious. That made her glance back over at the man. Now he was standing to his full height as he continued to consider the T-shirts. He was tall, and she could see just how well built he was.

She tilted her head, thinking there was something about him that was oddly famil-iar, although she had yet to see his features. Like her, he was wearing sunglasses. His were aviators. And even from a distance she could tell he was an American. He had chocolate-colored skin, and his dark hair was cut close to his head.

"Delicious, miss?"

She glanced back at the woman and smiled, remembering they were talking about the strawberries and not the man. "Yes, definitely delicious."

"Would you like another?"

Darcy chuckled. She hadn't intended on being greedy but since the woman asked . . . "Yes, I'd love another."

She put another strawberry into her mouth, and when she glanced back over at the man, she saw he was staring over at her. Facing him, she immediately recognized him and almost choked on the strawberry in her mouth.

York Ellis!

Even wearing sunglasses she would know him anywhere. The shape of his mouth and his chiseled jaw would give him away each time. What the heck was he doing here?

She felt irritation invade her entire body. Staring into his handsome face did nothing to calm her rising anger. Her best friend was married to one of his godbrothers, so they were usually invited to the same family functions.

She and York always managed to rub each other the wrong way whenever they would run into each other. Things had been that way between them since the time they'd met at Ellie and Uriel's wedding two years ago. During that time, her ex-husband Harold had tried threatening her to take him back. York had tried coming on to her at the reception. She had been in a bad mood at the time and had rebuffed his advances. Evidently he hadn't taken rejection well.

He removed his sunglasses and stood staring across the way at her, evidently as surprised to see her as she was to see him. She felt her body get hot under his intense stare but forced her emotions to stay in check. She certainly couldn't be that hard up for a man that she would be attracted to him.

And this wasn't just any man. It was York Ellis. He was arrogant. Cocky. Too damn sure of himself at times to suit her. So why was she having such a hard time dragging her gaze from him? Why instead was she allowing her eyes to roam all over him, taking in how well he fit his jeans, his shirt? And then, there was his looks . . .

So, okay he had a nice looking mouth, one that was shaped just for kissing and those other scandalous things mouths could do. And his eyes were dark, so compelling and so magnetic. And at the moment, those dark eyes were intent on staring her down.

His half smile told her he knew she was checking him out and evidently found it amusing, considering their history. Anyone who'd ever hung around them knew they had one. He rubbed her the wrong way, and it seemed she always managed to rub him the wrong way as well.

He continued to smile, and she tried to ignore the fact that doing so made the angular plane of his face more pronounced, made dimples slash deep in his cheeks. This was the first time she ever noticed them. But then this was the first time he'd smiled at her.

But she quickly reminded herself he wasn't smiling at her now. He was smirking at having caught her sizing him up. Good grief! With his arrogance, he'd probably assumed she was interested in him sexually — not on her life and not even if he was the last man on this earth.

But then she couldn't help noticing that he was checking her out as well. His gaze was scanning up and down her body, and in response she could feel the nipples of her breasts press hard against the material of her sundress. She broke eye contact to reach for another strawberry. She needed it.

"All the others are for sale, Miss," the woman told her gently.

30

Darcy couldn't help but chuckle at the woman's game and conceded it had worked. The woman had offered her two free strawberries to taste, knowing she would like them enough to buy the rest. And she was right.

"All right then, I want the entire basket. They are delicious."

The woman's face beamed. "Thank you. Would you like to try any other fruit?"

Darcy figured she might as well — anything to get her mind off the man across the street. Ellie liked York and couldn't figure out why her best friend and one of her husband's godbrothers could not get along. She had constantly told Ellie not to lose any sleep over it. Life wasn't intended for every single person to live together in harmony.

She glanced back at York and saw he was still staring over at her. Data rushed through her brain as to how much she knew about him. He was thirty-four, had gotten a criminology degree from a university in Florida and had been a cop with the NYPD for a few years before going into business for himself as a security expert. Both of his parents were living, and he had a younger sister and brother.

She also knew that he and his six godbrothers had formed the Bachelors in Demand club, with each one vowing to remain single. Now it was down to only four since two had married. Uriel Lassiter had married Ellie and Xavier Kane had married a woman by the name of Farrah earlier in the year.

"Here are your purchases," the woman said, handing her a huge brown paper bag containing the strawberries, mangoes and guineps. Darcy figured her next destination would be the hotel. Seeing York had practically ruined her day. She needed to revamp and get prepared for her night on the beach.

"Here, let me help you with that."

Darcy turned her head at the deep, husky male voice who'd spoken close to her ear at the same time her bag was smoothly taken from her hand. She frowned when she glanced up at a face that was too handsome for his own good. "York, what are you doing here in Jamaica?" She all but snapped the question out at him.

He smiled, and she had to force her gaze from the curve of his mouth when he said, "Funny, I was about to ask you the same thing. Are you sure New York can handle things without you?"

"It will be a struggle, but they'll manage," she responded smartly. They both lived in

New York but made it a point not to have their paths cross, which had always been fine with her — definitely preferable. "What about with you? Is the security of the city being tested with you gone?"

"Not at all," he said smoothly. "And you never answered my question as to what you're doing here in Jamaica."

She glared up at him. "Not that it's any of your business but I'm here vacationing for three weeks. I've earned the time off and intend to enjoy myself. And why are you here?"

"Vacationing as well. Funny we picked the same place to unwind and seek out relaxation."

Darcy didn't see anything amusing about it. Being on the same island with him was definitely not how she wanted things to be. It was bad enough that they lived in the same city. "Well, enjoy your vacation, and I can carry my own bag, thank you." She tried tugging her bag from his grip and he held tight.

"Excuse me, but will you let go of my bag?"

Instead of doing so, he asked, "Where are you on your way to?"

She let out a deep, frustrated sigh. "My hotel."

"Which one?"

"The Ritz-Carlton," she said, without thinking.

His smile widened. "Now isn't that a coincidence? So am I."

He had to be joking, she thought. There was no way he could be staying at her hotel. As if he'd read her thoughts, he chuckled and said, "I guess this isn't your lucky day, huh?"

She snatched her bag from him. "You're right, it's not."

She turned and thanked the woman for her purchase and moved to walk away. Why wasn't she surprised when York fell in step beside her? She stopped and turned to him. "And just where do you think you're going?"

"Back to the hotel. Since we're headed the same way, I figure we might as well keep each other company."

"Has it ever occurred to you that I might not want your company?"

His answer was simple. "No, that thought has never occurred to me."

"Like the time you rushed over to my place thinking I was a helpless female in distress?"

He laughed. "Hey, that was Ellie's idea, not mine."

He was right. It had been Ellie's idea. She and Ellie had been talking on the phone late one night when Darcy had heard a noise downstairs. She put Ellie on hold to investigate, not knowing Ellie had panicked and called York, who lived less than a mile away. Ellie had asked him to go to Darcy's house to make sure everything was okay.

It turned out there had been a burglar. Some guy had broken into her house, and she had caught him rummaging through her kitchen drawers. By the time York had gotten there, the guy had discovered just how well she could defend herself when she'd demonstrated the karate skills she'd acquired growing up and taking classes with her brothers.

York, who had arrived before the police, had gotten extremely angry with her, saying she had no business taking on the likes of a burglar. Of course, she had disagreed with him.

"Okay, your showing up at my place might have been El's idea, but you had no right to scold me in front of those police officers."

"You took your life in your hands when you should have called the police," he said, and she could tell from the tone of his voice her actions that night last year was still a sore spot with him.

"Had I waited for the police, the man would have gotten away just to break into someone else's home. I had no intentions of letting him do that."

York frowned. "Does it matter that you could have gotten killed?" Anger laced his every word.

"Could have but I didn't. I had sized up the situation and knew it was one I could handle. Not every woman needs a man for protection, York."

"And evidently you're one of those kinds."

She wasn't sure what he meant by that, but hell yes, she was one of those kinds. She didn't need a man around to protect her. Her first husband had learned that the hard way when he began showing abusive tendencies. "I guess I am," she finally said, smiling as if she was proud of that fact.

She began walking again, convinced he would decide he wouldn't want her company after all. He proved her wrong when he picked up his pace and began walking beside her again. She decided to ignore him. The good thing was that the hotel was less than a block away.

York walked beside Darcy and tried not to keep glancing over at her. She looked cute in her wide-brimmed straw hat and sundress. He had noticed her checking him out, and when she'd removed her sunglasses and he'd seen it was Darcy, he hadn't known whether to be amused or annoyed. She certainly hadn't known who he was at first, just like he hadn't recognized her.

But once she had known it was him, he could immediately see her guard go up. She had intended to put distance between them. At any other time he would let her but not this time. He wasn't sure why, but all he knew was that was how it would be.

"Would the lady like to look at my bracelets?" a peddler asked.

She stopped and so did York. He observed her when she conversed with the man who had several bangle bracelets for her to see.

York continued to watch as the man ardently pitched his goods and was impressed with the way Darcy handled the anxious merchant by not giving in to his outrageous prices. He inwardly chuckled, thinking she definitely had no intentions of paying an exorbitant amount.

She seemed pretty sharp for a twenty-eight-year-old, and he figured she rarely missed anything. It would be hard, if not next to impossible, for a man to run a game on her.

He could vividly recall the first time he'd

seen her rushing into the church for Uriel's wedding rehearsal. She'd been late since her plane had had mechanical problems.

Like all the other men, he had simply stared at her — the woman with all that dark brown hair flowing around her shoulders, hazel eyes, striking cocoa-colored features and a body to die for. The last thing he'd expected when he'd tried coming on to her later was to be told she wasn't interested. He would admit it had been a blow to his ego. That incident had been almost two years ago, and if the way she'd been sizing him up moments ago was anything to go by, it seemed she was pretty interested now.

He knew he should let go and move on, but so far he hadn't been able to do that. And whenever he saw her they had a tendency to get on each other's last nerves. If the truth be told, he had a mind to pay her back for rebuffing his advances that day. He could seduce her, make love to her and then walk away and not look back. Yes, that would serve her right.

"Well, that's that," she said, reclaiming his attention. He saw the way her lips quirked in amusement as well as the gleam of triumph shining in her eyes. He gathered she'd made a purchase she was pleased with.

They continued walking again, side by side, and he wondered how long she would continue to ignore him. He decided to stir conversation and asked, "When was the last time you talked to Ellie?" He eased the bag containing her fruit from her hand once again.

Darcy glanced over at York and decided that she would allow him to carry that bag since he seemed hell-bent on doing so anyway. She would keep the bag with the four bracelets she'd purchased from the peddler at a good price. "We're best friends, so I talk to El practically every day," she said. "But she hasn't called since I arrived here. She's going to be busy this week."

"Doing what?"

She wondered if he thought everything was his business. "She's hosting several holiday parties."

"Oh."

"It is the holiday season, you know," she reminded him.

"Yes, I know."

She didn't say anything and for a moment regretted bringing up any mention of the holidays. She'd heard from El that a woman York had been dating and had begun caring deeply about, and who'd been a fellow officer when he'd been a cop with the NYPD, had gotten gunned down on Christmas Day while investigating a robbery. That had been over six years ago. After that, he'd sworn never to get seriously involved with a woman again, especially one in a dangerous profession. She knew all about the Bachelors in Demand club, one he formed along with his bachelor godbrothers who were all intent on staying single men forever. She had met all six of the godbrothers and got along with each of them . . . except for York.

"So how are your parents?" she asked, deciding to change the subject. She had first met the Ellises at Ellie and Uriel's wedding and had run into them again when another one of Uriel and York's godbrothers, Xavier Kane, had gotten married earlier in the year.

"They're doing fine. I visited with them a couple of months ago." He glanced back over at her. "So what do you plan on doing later?"

She glanced up at him from under the wide-brimmed hat. "I'm resting up for the big beach party the hotel is hosting tonight. I hear it's a real classy black-tie affair. You are going, aren't you?"

"Hadn't planned on it."

"Oh, well." She should have felt relieved that he wouldn't be there, but for some reason she felt a pang of disappointment in her chest. Why was that?

"Behave yourself tonight, Darcy."

She lifted a brow. If he was being cute, she wasn't appreciating it. "Let me assure you, Mr. Ellis, that you don't need to tell me how to behave. And just for the record, I don't plan on taking your advice. The reason I'm here is to have a good time, and a good time is what I will have — even if it means misbehaving."

He stopped walking and stared at her, and she could see anger lurking in the dark depths of his eyes. She knew it was probably bothering him that she was standing there, facing him and looking nonplussed. Her two brothers were dominating males, so York's personality type was not foreign to her. But that didn't mean she had to tolerate it or him.

She glanced around. They were now standing in the plush lobby of the hotel. "I guess this is where we need to part ways, and hopefully we won't run into each other again anytime soon. You didn't say how long you intend to visit here."

He smiled at her. "No, I didn't say."

And when she saw that he had no intention of doing so either, she released a sigh, took her bag from him and said, "Goodbye, York." She then turned and headed for the bank of elevators.

Darcy drew in a deep breath with every step she took, tempted to glance over her shoulder. But she had a feeling he was still standing there, staring at her, and she didn't want to give him the impression that she'd given him another thought . . . although she was doing so.

A few moments later, she stepped on the elevator and turned. She'd been right. He was still standing there. And while others joined her on the elevator their gazes held. At that moment, she felt a pang of regret that the two of them had never gotten along. Too bad. She was too set in her ways to make any changes now. Besides, she didn't want to make any changes. For some reason, she much preferred that she and York keep their distance. The man was temptation personified. She could deal with temptation but not when it included an extreme amount of arrogance.

The elevator doors swooshed shut, breaking their eye connection. She released a deep breath, only realizing at that moment she'd been holding it. He was staying in another section of the hotel. It was a humongous place, but their paths might cross again and she would be ready and prepared.

She had no intentions of letting York Ellis catch her off guard again.

CHAPTER 2

Damn, the woman was too beautiful for her own good, York thought, watching the elevator door close behind Darcy Owens. Beautiful with a smart mouth, a delectable looking mouth. More than once he'd been tempted to kiss it shut and to demonstrate just what he could do when his tongue connected with hers.

But then he had to remember that Darcy was too brash and outspoken to suit him. He didn't want a "yes" woman by any means, but he didn't want a woman who would dissect his every word looking for some hidden meaning. For some reason, she couldn't take things at face value when it came to him, and he couldn't understand why.

If he had the time, he would put it at the top of his list to seduce the smart-mouthed Darcy Owens just for the hell of it. If she wanted to misbehave, he could certainly show her what misbehaving was all about. But he had to remember she was the best friend of his godbrother's wife, and Ellie probably wouldn't take too kindly if he seduced her best friend just for the hell of paying her back.

He was about to head over to his side of the hotel when his cell phone rang. He pulled it off his belt and saw it was Wesley Carr, one of the retired police officers that he used as part of his investigative team. It had been his father's idea.

Jerome Ellis had retired a few years ago as a circuit judge. He was a firm believer that retired police officers could better serve as more than just bailiffs at the courthouses. Most had sharp minds and loved the challenge of working on a case. York had taken his father's advice and hired three such men at his firm and never regretted doing so.

"Yes, Wesley, what you got for me?" York asked.

"First of all, are you taking those vitamin supplements I told you about?" Wesley asked.

York shook his head. One of the pitfalls of hiring the men was that they liked to run his life by making sure he got the proper rest, ate healthy and didn't overdo it when it came to women. They claimed all three things would eventually take a toll on a man.

"Yes, I'm taking them, so what do you have?"

"I think Damien Felder might be your man," Wesley said with certainty.

"Why?"

"He has a ton of gambling debts."

York rubbed his chin thoughtfully. "He's a gambler?"

"Of the worse kind. Although he's tried covering his tracks, I was able to trace his ties to the Medina family."

"Damn." The Medina family had their hands into anything illegal they could touch. York hadn't gotten wind of them involved in movie piracy before now, though. Mainly it'd been drugs, prostitution and the transportation of illegal immigrants.

And Roswell Medina's name had been linked to the homicide investigation involving Rhona, the only woman York had ever considered marrying. Like him she had been a police officer and had gotten struck down by a bullet when she had investigated a robbery. The authorities believed the rash of burglaries in Harlem had been organized by Medina but could never prove it.

"I can see them getting interested, if they had the right person on the inside to help them. It's evidently a profitable business,"

46

York added.

"Apparently."

He inhaled a deep sigh. He knew Damien Felder would be the one to watch for a while. "I want all the information you can get me on Felder's association with any of the Medinas." He would just love to nail any member of that crime family for something, even if it was for jaywalking.

As he headed back toward his side of the hotel he thought about Darcy and doubted the two of them would be running into each other again any time soon.

Hell, he hoped not.

A twenty-piece orchestra on the beach.

The hotel had thought of everything, Darcy concluded as she stepped outside. Everyone had been told that tonight's affair was all glitz and glamour, and everyone had dressed to the nines. Men were in tuxes and women were in beautiful gowns. She had decided to wear the short white lace dress and silver sandals she had purchased a few months ago when she had joined Ellie on a shopping spree when she'd visited her best friend in Charlotte.

With a glass of champagne in her hand, Darcy made her way down the white stone steps with towering balustrades on both sides. She could see the beach and see how the water was shimmering beneath the glow of the moon. To her right, tables of food had been set up, and shrimp, lobsters and oysters were being steamed on an open fire.

For those not wanting to get sand in their shoes, a huge wooden deck had been placed on the ground, and several light fixtures provided just the right amount of light to the affair.

She was about to grab another flute of champagne from a passing waiter when she happened to glance across the way and saw a man looking at her. He looked American and she placed his age in his late thirties. And she had to give it to him — he looked like a million bucks in his black tux.

But compared to York there was something lacking. He was handsome, although he wasn't of the jaw-dropping kind like York Ellis. And she would have to be the first to concede that even with all the stranger's handsomeness, she couldn't even conjure up what hero he could represent from those tons of romance novels she had read. She'd had no such problem with York.

She bit down on her lip wondering why she'd just made the comparison. Why had York even crossed her mind? The stranger smiled over at her, and she smiled back before another partier walked up to him and claimed his attention. At least it hadn't been a woman. As she sipped her champagne, she saw him glance over her way, as if assuring himself she was still there — still unattached, possibly still interested.

Deciding not to appear too interested, she began mingling, enjoying the sights and sounds. Moments later, she was leaning against a balustrade watching a group of the island dancers perform. Their movements were so romantic and breathtaking beneath the stars.

"I can tell you are enjoying yourself," a deep, husky male voice said.

The first thought that flashed through her mind was that it wasn't as deep as York's, and it wasn't making her skin feel like it was being caressed. Pushing that observation to the back of her mind, she looked up at the stranger she'd seen earlier and asked, "And just how can you tell?"

"You have that look. And whatever the cause of it, do you mind sharing it because I'm simply bored."

She fought from shaking her head. She had heard that pickup line so many other times, surely the man could have thought of something else. But she could go along with it for now. "Then I guess I need to make sure you enjoy yourself as much as I do."

He smiled, flashing her perfect white teeth. "I would definitely appreciate it." He then held his hand out to her. "I'm Damien Felder, by the way."

She returned his smile. "And I'm Darcy Owens."

"Please to meet you, Darcy. And is that a Midwestern accent I hear?"

"Yes, it is," she replied. "And yours is part southern and part western."

Instead of saying whether her assumption was correct, he took a step closer to her. "Are you staying at this hotel?"

She didn't have to wonder why he was asking. The man was a fast mover, and she had no problem with that if her vibes had been in sync with his. They weren't for some reason. "Yes, I'm at this hotel. What about you?"

"No, my hotel is a few miles from here. I was invited tonight by a friend. But an emergency came up, and he had to leave the island. He encouraged me to come anyway. He thought I would enjoy myself. I hadn't been until I saw you."

She smiled. "Thank you."

"You're welcome. And why would a beautiful woman travel to this island alone?"

She took a sip of her champagne and

smiled as she looked up at him. "What makes you think I'm alone?"

A gleam appeared in the depths of his brown eyes. "Because no man with a lick of sense would let you out of his sight for long."

Darcy smiled. The man was full of compliments, although she'd heard most of them before. "I needed a little vacation." And before he could ask her anything else, she decided to ask him a question. "So what brings you to the island?"

"I'm associated with a movie that will be filmed on the island starting tomorrow."

She lifted a brow. "A movie?"

He chuckled. "Yes, one from Spirit Head Productions."

She nodded. She had heard of them. In fact, their main headquarters were in New York. "Let me guess," she said smiling. "You're the leading man."

From his expression, she could tell he enjoyed getting compliments as much as he enjoyed giving them. "No, I hold an administrative position. I'm a line producer."

"Sounds exciting."

He met her gaze. "It is. How would you like me to give you a tour of the set tomorrow?"

She thought his offer was certainly generous, and she could tell from the way he was looking at her he thought so too and expected her to jump at it. So she did, all but clapping her hands in fake excitement. "Oh, that would be wonderful. I'd love to."

"Well then, it's settled. Now how about if I come up to your room tonight so I'll know where to come get you tomorrow."

"I prefer that we meet in the lobby."

She could see the disappointment flash in his eyes. She all but shrugged at the thought. He might eventually share her bed before she left the island, but he would work hard for the privilege. So far she didn't feel a connection to him but was hoping it was just her and not him. For some reason when she looked at him, visions of York entered her mind. And that wasn't good.

"Would you like to take a walk on the beach?"

She smiled. "No. In fact, it's been a tiring day for me. I think I'll call it an early night and go back up to my room now," she said.

"Alone?" he asked.

"Yes, alone. I'm recovering from a flu bug and don't want to overdo it."

"I understand, and I wouldn't want you to overdo it either." He reached into his jacket and pulled out a card. "Here's my business card. Call me when you get up in the morning. Maybe we can share breakfast."

"Thanks, and I will give you a call," she said, taking the card.

"Are you sure you don't need me to walk you back to your room?"

"Thanks for the offer but I'm positive. Good night. I'll see you tomorrow, Damien."

And then she walked off, knowing he was still watching her. She knew he thought he had her within his scope, but he would soon discover that she was the one who had him in hers.

York stood in the shadows, behind the orchestra stand, and sipped his wine. He watched the man he'd identified earlier that day as Damien Felder, hitting on Darcy Owens of all people. And from the way the man was still looking at Darcy as she disappeared among the other partiers, he was definitely interested in her. That York could understand. Not only did she have striking features but the dress she was wearing showed a pair of gorgeous legs and a very curvy body.

"Damn." He drew in a deep breath. The man's interest in Darcy was the last thing York needed. Based on the report Wesley had given him earlier, Felder was the last person she should even be talking to. Even Malcolm and his group didn't know half the stuff Damien Felder was involved in, but York didn't plan on sharing any of it with them until he had concrete proof to back it up.

But first he needed to make sure Darcy stayed out of the picture. He had seen the moment Felder had slid his business card into the palm of her hand. Since York could read lips — something he taught himself to do after his sister was born deaf — he knew that Felder had invited her on set tomorrow. He wasn't sure what her response had been since Felder had been the one facing him, while Darcy's back had been to him.

The man had also tried inviting himself up to Darcy's room, which she apparently turned down since she had left the party alone. At least York was grateful for that. He felt a deep pull in his stomach and tried convincing himself that the only reason he was grateful was because he was looking out for her. After all, she was Ellie's best friend, so that was the least he could do. Wanting to keep her out of the picture had nothing to do with the jealousy he'd felt when he'd seen Felder approach her. He assured himself that it hadn't been jealousy, just concern. Besides, too much was at stake with this case, and the last thing he needed was Darcy screwing things up.

He was about to leave when he noticed Felder giving the nod to another woman at the party. He recognized her immediately — Danielle Simone, the leading lady in the movie they were filming. Malcolm was pretty convinced that Danielle was not in any way a part of the black market ring. Now York wasn't so sure when he watched as she walked toward the beach with Felder following her, keeping a careful distance.

Interesting. He couldn't help wonder what that was about. Were the two having a secret affair? His cell phone rang, and he picked it up. It was one of his men who was attending the party undercover. "Yes, Mark, I picked up on the two. Follow them from here, and let me know where they go and what they do."

He clicked off the phone, satisfied his man was on it and wouldn't let the couple out of his sight. York then turned toward the part of the hotel where Darcy's room was located.

Darcy had showered and slipped into the hotel's complimentary bathrobe when she heard a knock on her hotel room door. She frowned, wondering who it could be. It was way past midnight, although she was sure a number of people were still at the party having a good time.

She crossed the room to look out the peephole in the door, and a frown settled around her mouth. *York Ellis.* Why on earth would he visit her room, and most importantly, how did he know her room number? She knew for certain that she had not given it to him.

Knowing he was the only person who could answer that question, she tightened the belt around her robe before taking off the lock and snatching open the door. "York, what on earth are you doing here, and how do you know my room number?"

"We need to talk."

"What?" she asked as she nearly drowned in the dark eyes staring down at her. She'd always thought they were such a gorgeous pair — although she would never admit such a thing to him or anyone else for that matter. She wouldn't even confess it to Ellie. Nor would she ever mention how heat would course through her body whenever he stood this close to her. She'd noticed it that first time they'd met, which was why she had deliberately avoided him. The last thing she had needed at the time was to be attracted to a man after what she'd gone through with her ex-husband.

"I said we need to talk, Darcy."

She stiffened her spine and glared at him. "Why? And you haven't answered my question. How did you get my room number?"

He leaned in the doorway, and her gaze watched his every movement at the same time her nostrils inhaled his manly scent. Her heart skipped a beat when her gaze roamed over him. He looked good in a tux. Had he attended the party when he'd said earlier that day that he wouldn't be doing so?

"I have ways of finding out anything I want to know, Darcy."

The deep huskiness of his voice had her gaze returning back to his. Even leaning in the doorway, he was towering over her. For some reason, her gaze shifted to his hands. This wasn't the first time she had noticed just how large they were. Heat spread throughout her body when she recalled the theory about the size of a man's hands and feet in comparison to another part of his anatomy. Automatically her gaze shifted to his feet.

"Looking for anything in particular?"

She snatched her gaze up to him. He had caught her checking him out again. "No, I was just thinking." That wasn't a total lie. He didn't have to know what she was thinking about. "And as far as you having ways of finding out whatever you want to know . . . well, that's probably true, but you won't hold a single conversation with me unless you tell me what it's about."

He rubbed his hand down his face as if annoyed with her. "It's about Damien Felder. You were flirting with him at the party tonight."

They were flirting with each other, but his impression of how things had been meant nothing to her. "I thought you weren't going to the party."

"I changed my mind."

"And you know Damien?"

He shook his head. "No, but I know *of* Damien, which is what I want to talk to you about."

There was no denying that York had her curious. "Very well, come in."

She took a step back, and he entered her hotel room and closed the door behind him. He glanced around the room, and when his gaze returned to her, it seemed the intensity in the depths of his eyes was pinning her in place.

She drew in a deep breath, refusing to get caught like a deer in the headlights where he was concerned. So she tightened the sash of her robe around her even more and broke eye contact with him and beckoned him to the sofa. "Have a seat and let's talk."

She watched him move to the sofa while heat spread throughout her body. He looked too darn comfortable for her liking. There was something about the way he was sitting, with his arms spread across the back of the sofa, that made her want to slide down on the sofa with him, ease the tux jacket off his shoulders and run her hands across the broad width of his chest.

Where on earth had those thoughts come from? This was York Ellis, the one man she didn't get along with, the one man who seemed to enjoy rubbing her the wrong way whenever their paths crossed. "What about Damien?" she spoke up and asked, reminding herself the only reason he was sitting on her sofa was because she was interested in what he had to say.

For some reason, the mention of Damien made him lean closer, cause something akin to anger to flash across his features. "You met him tonight."

She heard the censure in his tone and wondered the reason for it. "Yes, and why do you care?"

Evidently her question stumped him. The

irritation in his face was replaced by a slow smile, one that didn't quite reach his eyes. "Personally, I don't other than the fact that you're screwing things up for me and my investigation."

She bit down on her lips as she struggled to keep a civil tongue. "What investigation?"

As he sat back, York drew in a deep breath, trying to calm the anger that was flowing through him. And it was anger he could not explain. What she did and who she did it with was her business. He shouldn't care one bit, and he had tried convincing himself that he didn't. But the truth of the matter was that he did. There was no way he would allow her to blindly walk into a dangerous situation.

"I wasn't absolutely up front with you earlier today when I gave my reason for being here on the island."

"You weren't?"

"No. I'm here on a job. My company was hired by a group of moviemakers for security detail on a movie being filmed, the same one Felder is associated with. And while my outfit is doing that, I'm working behind the scenes to protect their interest. Someone is slipping the movies to the black market before their theatrical release."

She lifted a brow. "And what does that

have to do with Damien Felder?"

It was hard to explain why a part of him wanted to kiss her and strangle her at the same time. What was there about her that could drive him to such extremes? "I have reason to believe Felder might be involved in some way."

"Do you have any proof?"

"No."

"Then it's merely speculation on your part."

"For now. But he is being watched, and if he is guilty, I would hate for your name to be linked to his."

She glared at him. "And what if your suspicions are wrong? Do you expect me not to enjoy the company of a man because you think he might be involved in some case you're investigating?"

"I was hoping that you would. And as far as me suspecting him, I'm almost sure he's my man. I wouldn't have come to you if I didn't."

Darcy wondered just why he had. They weren't friends, so his concern about her had nothing to do with it. He must have been truthful earlier when he'd said she had the potential of screwing things up for him.

She stood. "Okay, you've warned me. I'll walk you to the door."

He remained sitting. "And what the hell does that mean?" he asked.

The anger in his tone made her lift her chin. "It means just what I said, York. You've warned me. Now you can leave."

"But you will take my advice."

To Darcy, it sounded more like a direct order than a question. "No, I don't plan to take your advice. Unless you have something more concrete than assumptions, I see no reason not to see Damien again. In fact, we've made plans for later today."

He held her gaze, and she could see the fire in his eyes. He was so angry with her that he was almost baring his teeth. He slowly leaned forward in his seat, and in a tone of voice tinged with a growl, he asked, "Why are you being difficult?"

She curved her lips into a smile only because she knew it would get on his last nerve. "Because I want to."

She knew she was being childish. Pretty darn petty, in fact, when for whatever his reason, he had come to warn her about Damien. She had no intentions of telling him that the warning was not needed since she wasn't attracted to Damien and didn't plan on seeing him again after their date that day. And the only reason she was keeping her date with him was because she'd always wanted to check out a movie set, nothing more. Even with Damien's handsome looks, he hadn't done anything for her.

And definitely not in the way the man sitting on her sofa was doing. Even now she was struggling, trying hard to fight the attraction, the magnetic pull, especially since it was an attraction she didn't want or need. And it was an attraction she didn't intend to go anywhere.

"You like rattling me, don't you, Darcy?"

His words pulled her attention back to the present. She figured there was no need to lie. "Yes, I guess I do."

Darcy didn't think there could be anything sexy about a man who merely stood up from sitting on a sofa. But with York, watching his body in movement was enough to cause heat to flare in her center and the juncture of her thighs.

And when he slowly walked toward her, advancing on her like he was the hunter and she his prey, she merely stood her ground. She refused to back up or retreat. And it seemed he had no intentions of halting his approach until he came to a stop in front of her.

"I've heard of stubborn women before, but you have to be the stubbornest."

She glared up at him. "I'll take that as a compliment, York. Now if you don't mind, it's late and you need to leave."

York thought some women had to be born for trouble, and this one standing in front of him was one of them. Against his better judgment, he had come here tonight to give her fair warning and he had done so. If she didn't want to heed to his warnings, there was nothing he could do about it.

He tried to push the thought from his mind that while he'd been sitting on the sofa, whether she knew it or not, he had been fighting desire for her that had all but seeped into his bones. Why on earth would he be attracted to her of all women?

Before he'd come up to her room tonight, he'd been approached by a couple of women who'd all but invited him to their hotel room. One had brazenly offered to give him a blow job right there on the elevator. But he hadn't wanted any of them. He wanted this one. This haughty looking female, who had blood firing through his veins, who was staring him down and standing in front of him looking as sexy as any woman had a right to look in a bathrobe.

He glared down at her when the room got too quiet for his taste. "Don't say I didn't warn you."

"I won't. Now goodbye, York."

At that moment, something inside of him snapped. She was glaring at him, yet earlier tonight she'd been smiling at Damien Felder. Not only had she been smiling but she'd also flirted with the man. "You like pushing my buttons, don't you, Darcy?"

"Yes," she said smiling. "Gives me great pleasure."

"No, this is pleasure." And then he reached out, pulled her to him and captured her mouth with his.

CHAPTER 3

He was right, Darcy thought, when York began kissing her with a hunger that surprised her. This was pleasure. And it began overwhelming her as sensations tore through her. When she felt those big hands she'd checked out earlier tighten their hold on her, she became wrapped in his heat with every languorous stroke of his tongue. That was all it took for desire to start coiling deep in her body, thickening the blood rushing through her veins. And when she released a surprised gasp, he slid his tongue deeper inside her mouth.

He shifted, and his body pressed hard against her and she felt him — his aroused thickness. His hardness. It was poking her in the belly. A part of her wanted to push him away. But another part wanted to draw him even closer. She knew what part won when a moan flowed from deep within her throat. Instinctively, she eased up on tiptoes to return the kiss with the same demand and hunger he was putting into it. And when her tongue tried battling his for control, his arms tightened even more around her, almost crushing her body to his. Easing upward shifted his aroused part from her belly right to the juncture of her thighs, and immediately she could feel her panties get wet.

York's heart was hammering hard in his chest. He didn't understand why he was kissing Darcy this way, a woman he'd convinced himself that he didn't even like. Evidently his personal feelings toward her had nothing to do with lust, and he was convinced that was what was filling his mind at that moment. That was what had him eating away at her mouth as if it was the last meal he would have. And she was kissing him back with just as much intensity. It seemed as if a floodgate had burst open, and they didn't know how to stop the lusty water from rushing through.

They didn't know or they didn't want *to know?*

At that moment, it didn't matter to him, and he had a feeling it didn't matter to her either. He wanted her, and from the way she was kissing him back, she wanted him as well. And if she didn't let up on his tongue he was certain he was going to lose his mind. He hadn't made love to a woman in a while, and he couldn't recall one being this passionate, this aggressive, this damn hot. He had initiated the kiss, but there was a big question as to who was being seduced.

Suddenly, he pulled back, reached out and ripped the bathrobe off her body. Just as he thought, she was completely naked underneath.

"What do you think you're doing?" she asked, inhaling a deep breath of air.

He glanced over at her while tearing off his own clothes, not believing she had to ask. But just in case she had any intentions of suddenly deciding she didn't want this as much as he did, he stopped short of removing his slacks. Instead he reached out, pulled her to him and captured her mouth once more.

Darcy couldn't help the moan that eased from deep in her throat. Had it really been two years since she'd felt sensations like this? Sure, there'd been Bruce, but York was showing her that when it came to hot sex between a man and woman, there was nothing like the real thing. A sex toy couldn't compare.

She felt everything. The hardness of his erection was pressed against her center, the material of his tux was rubbing against her thigh causing all kinds of sensations to erupt within her. And when she felt those large hands of his stroke the soft skin of her backside, molding her cheeks closer to him, she couldn't do anything but surrender. He had blazed a fire that was consuming them both.

Knowing she was capitulating didn't sit too well with her, but every stroke of his tongue in her mouth was making her appreciate the benefits. The man didn't intend to hold anything back, and she decided at that moment, neither would she.

She'd had all intentions of having an island fling, so there was no stopping her now. Besides, this would be a one-night stand. She would merely use him to take the two-year edge off, since he seemed to know just what he was doing.

He broke off the kiss, and his gaze burned into hers as he kicked off his shoes before easing his pants and briefs down his legs all at once. Her breath got caught in her throat when her gaze lowered. Maybe that saying about the size of feet and hands in comparison to other parts of a man's body wasn't just a theory at all. It was a truth.

Her gaze moved back to his face, and she wasn't sure who made the first move — nor did she care. All she cared about was that she was in his arms again while he kissed her with a madness she felt to her toes. And she was convinced what they were doing was sheer madness. A thought entered her mind that maybe they should slow down and talk about it. Then she decided there was no need to waste time talking.

He tore his mouth from hers, and the look she saw in his eyes indicated his agreement. "I want to get inside you, Darcy."

He couldn't have said it any plainer than that, she thought. She went to him and then spread her hands out across his stomach. His skin felt hot beneath her fingers, and that same heat spread through her when she moved her hands lower. When her hand pressed against the thickness of his muscular thighs, she felt a stirring in the pit of her stomach. The intensity of it was almost frightening.

She was convinced the desire taking over her mind and her body had nothing to do with York per se but with the fact that he was a man. But not just any man. He was a red-hot, good-looking man who had the ability to shoot adrenaline up her spine in very high dosages.

And she couldn't discount the fact that she hadn't slept with a man in almost two years, not since moving to New York. Before then, thanks to her ex-husband, she had washed her hands of men. She found there was too much drama where they were concerned. Bruce had been given to her as a prank gift and she — who'd never considered using a sex toy before — had discovered in time of need he could be her best friend.

But now York was reminding her in a very explosive way that there was nothing like a flesh and blood male. Nothing like a real man breathing down your neck, kissing you, touching you, letting you touch him. And at that moment, it didn't matter one iota that the man causing her so much sumptuous turbulence was the one man she thought she didn't even like.

She might have regrets for her actions in the morning, but at that very moment, she wanted him, too. She wanted him inside of her.

Her breaths were coming out in tortured moans when she lowered her hand and touched his erection. Ignoring his masculine growl, she cupped him, loving the feel of his hardness in her hand, loving the heat of it. It was rock hard. Solid. Big. And when she began running her thumb over the shaft's head, wanting to feel the protruding veins beneath her fingertips, she felt him shudder in her hand.

She imagined in the deep recesses of her mind this same solid flesh sliding all the way inside of her and how her muscles would clench it, possess it, milk it for everything it was worth and then some. It had been a long time for her, way too long. She was greedy and wanted it all.

She glanced up at him, met his gaze through desire-glazed eyes and saw the state of his arousal in the dark eyes staring right back at her.

"Condom?" she asked him almost in a moan. When he nodded and made a move to step back, she had to release him and immediately felt the loss.

And then he took time to remove his socks before retrieving a condom packet from his wallet. As if having a woman watch him don a condom was the most natural thing, he proceeded to put on protection.

She was suddenly engulfed in strong arms when York swept her off her feet to carry her to the bedroom.

York could not recall when he'd wanted a woman this much. And why did that woman have to be Darcy Owens? He should find the very thought unsettling, but at the moment too much desire was running through his body to be concerned with emotions he wasn't used to.

He figured there had to be a full moon out tonight, or maybe there was something to that passion fruit he'd had at lunch. Regardless, tomorrow and the days that followed he was certain he would be back on track — revert to his right mind and be ruled by logic and less by lust. He shouldn't have any problems keeping his distance from Darcy during his remaining time on the island.

But at this very moment his thoughts, his actions were ruled by a yearning that had taken over his entire body. Deep down, he knew it was almost two years in the works. He had wanted her the first time he'd seen her at Ellie and Uriel's wedding. He had even warned his other godbrothers to keep their distance. And when she had snubbed him, told him in no uncertain words that she wasn't interested, his attraction had turned to outright dislike. He hadn't taken her rejection well.

That's why one of the most satisfying things for him right now was to know she was as much of a goner as he was. She definitely wasn't rejecting him now. The thought made him smile as he placed her on the bed and then took a step back. See-ing her naked body in the middle of the king-size bed made him more aroused, especially when the mass of dark brown hair looked in total disarray around her shoul-ders. She looked sexy. She looked hot. She looked as if she was ready for anything he had to give her. And tonight he had plenty.

But she intended to play the vixen. He figured as much when she deliberately stretched to make her breasts lift at an angle that made them appear ready for his mouth. And her legs slowly opened, showing how ripe, wet and ready she was. A fierce need ripped through him, and he moved back toward the bed. He was well aware of the rules he would be breaking about never los-ing control when it came to a woman.

He chuckled. It was too late. He'd already lost it. And he would make sure that her payback for driving him over the edge was a night she wouldn't forget. He knew for certain that he wouldn't.

York moved toward the bed, and his main thought was to reconnect his mouth to hers. He pulled her toward him and captured her mouth. There was something about her taste that had him wanting more. But she seemed just as ravenous as he and was returning his stroke lick for lick.

He broke off the kiss and lowered his gaze from her wet lips down her breasts, and he saw how her nipples were hardening to stiff buds right before his eyes. He felt all his senses begin to flash and his tongue all but thicken in his mouth with thoughts of just what he wanted to do with those nipples.

"You want to taste them, York? If so, don't let me stop you."

Her words had him glancing up. She must have seen the intensity in his gaze when he'd been staring at her breasts. He found a woman who spoke her mind in the bedroom pretty refreshing. But then he wasn't surprised that was the tactic an outspoken woman like Darcy would use.

His gaze lowered back to her nipples. Yes, he wanted to taste them. He was getting harder just thinking about all the things he'd liked doing to them with his mouth. But he wouldn't stop at her breasts. He intended to taste every inch of her and felt he should at least warn her.

"Your breasts aren't the only thing I want to taste, Darcy." He didn't feel he had to go into specifics. And just the thought rocked his senses.

York immediately drew a turgid nipple into his mouth and began devouring it with a greed he knew she'd feel all the way to her toes but especially at her center. And speaking of her center . . .

His hand found its target at the juncture of her thighs, and sensations sizzled through him, making him ache. His fingers spread her apart first, then delved into her heated wetness, and he felt his erection throb in response.

She moaned when he allowed his mouth to pay homage to the other nipple, letting his tongue lap at it a few times before easing it between his lips. He sucked on it while a lusty rush filled him, obliterated his senses and sent a fierce need rushing through his bloodstream.

And when he couldn't hold back any longer, he pulled away from her breasts and went straight to the source of her heat. Lifting her hips, he lowered his mouth to her, intent on licking every inch of her and lapping up her dewy wetness, tasting her until he got his fill. He wanted every lusty cell in his body to be satisfied.

Darcy began trembling the exact moment she felt the heat of York's tongue ease inside of her, and it became nearly impossible to breathe. All she could do was whimper in pleasure. So she did. He knew what he was doing by using his tongue to stroke her. He was so skilled that it had her shaking from head to toe. He felt her shudders and was lapping up every single shiver.

She needed to grab hold of something, and the bedspread just wouldn't do. So she reached for his head instead. She held him steady, kept him in place, but the feel of his tongue moving inside of her was too much. Her fingers clenched the side of his head the moment her world exploded in a orgasm that detonated every part of her body.

And she heard herself call his name. It was a blazing rush from her lips, a satisfying ache that she felt when his tongue delved deeper, lapped harder. She was transformed into a mass of lusty mush, and it had to be the most exquisite feeling she'd ever encountered. This single act was worth the two years she'd gone without.

When she felt him release her and pull out his tongue, she almost screamed her regret. Watching through passion-glazed eyes, she saw him straddle her, felt the hardness of him replace his tongue to ease inside of her, stretching her to the point where she wondered if they would fit and knowing he would die trying.

As if her body was made just for him, her insides expanded, got wetter, felt slicker. He continued to push his way inside, and she gazed up at him, saw the beads of perspiration on his brow. He lifted her hips, intent on her taking him, receiving him and welcoming him.

When he had reached her hilt, he began moving, stroking her with a rhythm that had every cell in her body, every single molecule responding. The heat of his skin rubbed against her thighs as he thrust back and forth, going deeper and deeper with every stroke. Her clit was on fire, and he wasn't trying to put out the flames. Instead, he was taking the flames higher, sparking every single ember inside of her.

And she clenched him, refusing to let him take without giving. She began milking him and felt her muscles tighten then pull to get the full benefit, maximize the sensual effect of what he was doing to her. The bed was shaking in its frame as he rode her in a way she'd never been ridden before. And his shaft seemed to get bigger and harder inside of her.

Just when she thought she couldn't take any more, she was pushed over the edge, and her body erupted in a colossal explosion. Her fingers dug into the muscles of his shoulders, and the lower part of her lifted off the bed with the massive blast. He growled when he pressed harder into her body, spreading her thighs apart even more.

York was replacing two years of pent-up, half-filled, half-measured pleasure. Before now what she'd assumed was satisfaction had only been appeasement. This was better than anything she could have imagined from any man or toy. It was beyond her wildest dream — and over the years she'd had plenty of wild dreams. But none could compare to this reality.

He continued to ride her, continued to pound into her, intent on getting in the last stroke, gratifying her every pulsation as well as his own.

"York . . ."

She heard the sound of his name from her lips as she continued to come, but she couldn't make herself stop as pleasure continued to hold her in its grip. She knew if she never made love to another man again she would have memories of tonight stored away in the back of her mind.

"Darcy . . ."

The rough and deep sound of his voice rushed over her, made her body respond the way it had never responded to a man before. She looked up into his dark gaze. He had slowed down but not stopped. And then he slowly began easing from her body when all of a sudden he thrust right back in all the way to the hilt. He lowered his head and whispered in her ear in a deep, primitive growl. "I want more."

And in response, she wrapped her legs around him as she felt need coupled with desire rush through her veins, overtake her senses. Tonight she would give him more because giving him more meant she was taking just as much for herself.

Daybreak was peeking through the window blinds when York glanced over his shoulder at Darcy. He slowly eased from the bed, determined not to wake her. Drawing in a deep breath, he tried to regain control of his senses while piecing together everything that had happened last night in this room. He should feel vindicated at having seduced her, but instead he was wondering who had seduced whom.

He'd known before last night there was sexual attraction between them, which was the cause of a lot of their bickering. But he hadn't known until last night just how much he'd wanted her — not just to prove a point or to right what he'd considered a wrong. He refused to think making love to her had anything to do with revenge or getting back at her. And he refused to consider the pleasure had been one-sided. She hadn't shown resistance to anything they'd done in that bed.

And hell, they had done a lot. He hadn't known a woman's skin could taste so luscious or that hazel eyes could turn so many different shades while in the throes of heated passion. Nor had he known that a woman could ride just as hard as a man.

Even when he had fought to keep himself in check and to regain control, he'd found his efforts wasted. Darcy had given him the kind of pleasure he hadn't shared with any woman before her. That said a lot, considering his reputation.

Before leaving her bedroom, he glanced over his shoulder. She was still sleeping, and he understood why. They had made love almost nonstop through the night. One orgasm was followed by another. The pleasure had been too intense to even think about stopping, and she hadn't complained. In fact, she had kept up with him all the way. At that very moment, he didn't see Darcy Owens as a woman with a smart mouth but as a woman who definitely knew how to use that mouth.

She was lying on top of the covers, and he couldn't stop his gaze from roaming over her naked body. Passion marks were visible on her thighs, stomach and around her breasts, and he could immediately recall the exact moment he'd placed each of them there. He shook his head and glanced down at himself. He had a number of passion marks on his body as well. Darcy definitely believed in equal play.

York glanced back at her and felt his body grow hard all over again. He drew in a deep breath and forced his gaze from her or else he'd be tempted to crawl back in bed with her, hold her in his arms and patiently wait until she awakened. Then he would make love to her all over again.

Damn. He was losing control again, becoming undone. Okay, he had enjoyed the Darcy experience, but he needed to regroup and remember the reason he was in Jamaica. And it wasn't to spend his time in Darcy Owens' bed.

But still, he wasn't sure if they understood each other where Damien Felder was concerned. She had started out defying him, and in the end, she still hadn't yielded to his way of thinking. He hoped what they shared last night gave her other ideas on the matter. He truly couldn't see how it couldn't.

And there was another thing he had to consider. He had gotten so into making love to her that he'd done something else he usually didn't do. He had taken risks by not putting on a new condom at the start of each lovemaking session. Although he wanted to believe it was a long shot, what if she was pregnant at this very moment?

Hell, York, don't even go there, man, a part of his mind screamed. *She's probably on the Pill, which means that although you got sloppy this one time, she managed to save the day . . . or in this case, the night.*

When she shifted her position in the bed he took a step back, feeling the need to put distance between them and knowing it would be best if he wasn't there when she woke up. There was no telling what frame of mind she would be in, and he didn't want her making it seem as though making love was all his idea. Nor did he want to hear that she regretted anything about their time together — especially when he had no regrets.

Once in her living room, he quickly picked up his clothes off the floor and put them on. He glanced at the clock on one of the tables and saw the time was six in the morning. Chances were he would be getting a lot of strange looks when he made his way from one part of the hotel to the other still wearing a tux. But then chances were anyone who saw him would figure out why. Liaisons were a way of life.

He crossed the room to glance into the bedroom once again before leaving. She was still sleeping like a baby, and as much as he wished otherwise, a part of him regretted that he wouldn't be there when she woke up.

CHAPTER 4

Darcy stirred awake when the sun spilled in through the window to hit her right in the face. But she refused to open her eyes just yet. She expected at any moment to feel York's warm breath on her neck or have his aroused body part — one that she'd gotten to know up close and personal — cuddle close to her backside, right smack against her bare cheeks. And she wouldn't mind it at all if he threw one of his legs over her. Nor would she care if he were to run his fingers through her hair.

But as she continued to lay there all she heard was silence and felt no human contact. Moments ticked by, and she flipped onto her back and glanced over at the empty spot beside her. Had York gotten up to use the bathroom?

Easing out of bed, she went into the bathroom and found it empty. She then strolled to the living room and found it vacant as well. Her bathrobe was tossed across the sofa, and his clothes that had littered the floor last night were gone. That meant he was wearing them.

Disappointment settled in her chest, and for a moment she wondered just what she had expected. York had handled last night for what it had been — a one-night stand. Why had she assumed he would think of it as anything more? Why did she care that he hadn't? And why was she taking it as a personal affront?

Both men and women had meaningless sexual liaisons all the time. She had even caught the plane from New York with plans to have a fling, had even joked with Ellie about it. But that was when she would have been in total control, and the man was to have been a stranger. Someone who wouldn't leave any lingering affects or someone she wouldn't miss once the moments passed. In other words, she hadn't expected York Ellis to be so overpowering, so overwhelming, so doggone good between the sheets that her body still throbbed between her legs.

She slid into her robe as she recalled her actions and behavior of the night. Red-hot embarrassment reddened her cheeks. She had gotten wild and outrageous. She guessed two years of celibacy could do that to you. And she didn't need to look at her body to know there were probably passion marks all over every inch of her skin. And she was certain he was sporting his fair share of the marks as well.

She ran her hands through her hair, frustrated. No matter how good the sex had been, she could literally kick herself for tumbling into bed with York. They didn't even like each other, although it was apparent they'd gotten along pretty well between the sheets. He had made her feel things she hadn't ever felt.

And after each lovemaking session, before they would start all over again, he would hold her tenderly in his arms. She certainly hadn't expected that. There had been something so calming and relaxing to lie there in his arms. And when she had dozed off to sleep that last time, weary after rounds and rounds of lovemaking, she had assumed he would be there whenever she woke up.

Wrong. He had skipped out like a thief in the night. It was hard to explain why she felt so annoyed about it but she was. His actions were probably his M.O. when it came to a woman. Why had she assumed things would be different with her?

Fine, he could continue to handle his

business that same way. It meant nothing to her. In fact, now that they'd gotten what they'd undoubtedly wanted from each other, she hoped she didn't run into him again while she was here. He wouldn't be the first man she'd written off.

Her marriage to Harold Calhoun had started out like a storybook romance. They had met in college and had married soon after graduation. But within a year after living under the same roof, she had discovered things about her husband she hadn't known — like the fact that he had a tendency to get abusive at times. The verbal abuse was bad enough, but the first time he'd tried getting physically abusive with her, it had been his last time. He had found out, much to his detriment, that his wife could defend herself so well, he'd been the one hovering in a corner pleading for mercy by the time the authorities had arrived.

She drew in a deep breath and turned toward her bedroom. She then recalled York's words to her about Damien Felder. As far as she was concerned, a man was innocent of any crime until proven guilty. Besides, she doubted had it been Damien who'd slept with her last night he would have left the way York had done, without even a wham, bam, thank you ma'am.

And speaking of Damien . . .

It was probably too late to join him for breakfast, but she would keep her date with him to let him show her around the movie set. She was a big girl who could handle herself, regardless of what York thought. And frankly, what he thought didn't matter to her.

She would arrange to meet Damien just as she'd planned. She had gotten what she wanted from York, and she was confident he'd gotten what he wanted from her. They were even. Now things could go back to how they'd always been between them.

York glanced around the movie set. Today the location was a cottage on the beach where the scene would be shot. The crew and equipment were in place, and the cast was in their individual trailers getting the attention of the hair and makeup artists.

He had been introduced earlier and was told his job was to provide backup security to the production team since they would be filming in several parts of the island, some less than desirable.

Several members of his security group would keep that focus while others worked undercover to identify who was crippling the production in another way. So far

Damien Felder hadn't shown up on set, and York hadn't missed the whispered jokes of several crew members as to why. A number were wondering whose bed he'd spent the night in. Evidently, Felder was a known playboy. So far, no one had linked Felder's name with that of the leading lady, and York found that slightly odd since very few secrets survived on a movie set. Someone was working extremely hard to keep their affair a secret. He definitely found that interesting.

"Um, looks like Damien has been busy," someone whispered behind York, and he glanced up to see Damien walk in with Darcy at his side. At that moment, York discovered firsthand what it meant to see bloodred. What the hell was she doing here with him? Hadn't she listened to anything he'd told her about Felder last night?

And he could tell from the whispers behind him that many assumed she had been Felder's sleeping partner last night. He was tempted to turn around and tell them how wrong they were since she had been his. But just the thought that she was getting whispered about, by those who didn't even know her and who assumed false things about her, pissed him off to the point where he was fighting intense anger within him.

He continued to pretend to peruse documents on a clipboard while watching Felder show Darcy around. It was obvious he was trying to impress her, probably was working real hard to get into her bed tonight or to get her in his. The thought of either happening set York on edge, made him madder.

"Ellis, I need to introduce you to Felder," Bob Crowder, the production manager, said.

York glanced up. "Fine. Let's do it," he said, placing the clipboard aside and trying to keep the hardness from his tone.

They crossed the room to where Felder stood with Darcy by his side near a tray of coffee and donuts. He smelled her before he got within ten feet of her. Aside from the cologne she was wearing, she had a unique feminine scent that could probably drive men wild. He wondered if he was the only man who detected it and quickly realized he had reason to know it so well. Her aroma had gotten absorbed into his nostrils pretty damn good last night.

"Damien, I need to introduce you to the guy who owns the company we're using for security now," Crowder said, snagging Felder's attention.

Felder turned and gave York a once-over

before asking, "What happened to the other company that was hired?"

"Evidently, they didn't work out," York responded before Crowder could. Felder really was in no position to ask questions.

"And you think your outfit will be able to do a better job?" Felder asked.

York smiled, well aware that Darcy was staring at him, listening attentively. At least she hadn't let on that they knew each other, and he was grateful for that. "I *know* we'll do a better job." He figured his response sounded pretty damn confident, overly cocky to an extreme, but that sort of attitude was probably one Felder could relate to.

Felder proved him right when his lips curved into a smile. "Hey, York Ellis. I like you."

It was on the tip of York's tongue to respond that the feeling wasn't mutual. Instead, he said, "My job is not to get you to like me, Felder, but to make sure you and everyone else who're part of this production are safe."

York knew his statement was establishing his persona as a no-nonsense sort of guy. That's what he wanted. He'd heard Felder had a tendency to try and cozy up to those in charge so when he decided to break rules they would look the other way. It was good to let the man know up front he wouldn't allow it and not to waste his time trying to earn brownie points.

He then shifted his gaze from Felder to Darcy. "And you are?"

York knew Felder assumed he was asking for security reasons. Darcy opened her mouth to respond, but Felder beat her to the punch. "She's with me, Ellis, and her name is Darcy Owens. She's my guest."

York nodded as he glanced down at the clipboard in his hand. "Her name isn't on the list, Felder." He could tell from Felder's expression that the man didn't appreciate being called out on breaking one of the production rules about bringing visitors on set.

"I made her an exception," Felder said, smiling.

"There are no exceptions around here," York said, not returning the smile. "In the future, make sure all exceptions are cleared by me first."

He glanced over at Darcy and saw her glaring at him, actually saw a spark of fire in her eyes. He then turned to Crowder. "I need to check on a few other things around here."

"All right, come on," Crowder said, before

leading him away. York didn't say anything else to the couple, just merely nodded before walking off.

"He's not going to last around here long," Darcy heard Damien mutter as they watched York leave.

"Why do you say that?" she asked, curious to know. She felt York's annoyance at seeing her as well as his immediate dislike of Damien. It was funny how well she could read him.

"He's trying to throw his weight around much too soon. I'd heard the bigwigs were sending in some new guy to handle security, but I can tell he's not going to work out. I don't like the fact that he questioned anything about you when you were with me."

She shrugged. "I'm sure he was just doing his job."

It wasn't that she was taking up for York's brash behavior but she didn't want to do anything to blow whatever cover he had, although she still wasn't convinced Damien was someone he should be watching. York had his reasons for being here on the island and she had hers. She intended to have a good time and enjoy herself.

Damien gave her a tour of the set while telling her bits and pieces of what scenes they would be shooting. Every once in a while she would glance over to where York was standing and find him staring hard at her. She would stare back. It seemed things were back to normal with them.

At least they were to a degree. Since sharing a bed with him she felt an intimate connection that she didn't want to feel. She could no longer look at his large hands and wonder. Now she knew. She couldn't look at his mouth without remembering all the naughty things his lips and tongue could do. Even from across the room he was emitting a heat that could sear her. Knowing that was the last thing she wanted, she let out a deep sigh.

"What's wrong? Am I boring you?"

She glanced up and forced a smile at Damien. "No, in fact I'm a little overwhelmed by it all. The next time I go to a movie I'm going to appreciate all the behind-the-scenes things it took to bring the movie to the big screen."

"Now you know." He glanced at his watch. "How would you like to have lunch with me? And then I can take you back to your hotel, let you rest up a bit and then we can go out tonight. I heard there's a club that's a hot spot on the island. I would love to take you dancing."

His suggestion sounded good, and there was no reason she shouldn't have lunch with him or go dancing at the club. Her smile widened and she said, "That sounds wonderful. I'd love to."

Out of the corner of his eye, York watched Darcy leave with Felder, and his heart banged against his chest causing a deep, hard thump. What the hell was wrong with him? He had gone above and beyond by warning her about the man, yet she still was with him today. It was as if she'd deliberately ignored what he'd said about Damien Felder.

"Looks like Damien's got another looker." York turned around slowly to face the production's leading man, Johnny Rush. He'd officially met the man yesterday. "Yeah, looks that way," he said dryly, as if the thought of who Felder was with didn't interest him in the least.

He knew that Malcolm was convinced Rush and Danielle Simone were in no way involved in the bootlegging activity, but as far as York was concerned, there was still a possibility. At least he was suspicious of Simone since she and Felder had met up somewhere last night.

"I wonder where they met."

He studied the man's features. "Is there any reason you want to know?"

Johnny shook his head and chuckled. "No, in fact I'm happy for him. Maybe now he'll leave Danielle alone."

York couldn't help wondering why Rush felt the need to drop that information. Since he wasn't sure, he decided to play it out as much as he could. "I didn't know he and Ms. Simone had something going on."

He saw the frown settle on Johnny's face. "They don't. Damien thinks he's someone important with this outfit and has been trying to box her into an affair. But she's not interested in him."

York nodded and decided not to say that wasn't the way he'd seen things last night. "And that bothers you?"

The man met his gaze and held it. "Yes, I want Danielle for myself."

The man couldn't get any plainer than that. Again, York wondered what purpose Johnny had for revealing that . . . unless the man assumed York would develop a roving eye where Danielle Simone was concerned. He decided to quickly squash that idea. "Good luck. I know how it feels when a man truly wants a woman."

Johnny lifted a brow. "Do you?"

"Yes. There's a woman I'm all into back

in New York. She's the only woman for me."
He said the lie so Johnny wouldn't think he
was a threat.

"You engaged?" Johnny asked.

"Not yet. I'm thinking of popping the
question around the holidays," York lied
further. What he'd just told Johnny was a
whopper. There was no way he was thinking
about proposing to any woman around the
holidays.

"Hey man, congratulations. I'm thinking
about asking Danielle myself around the
holidays."

York lifted a brow. "Things are *that* serious between you two?"

Johnny beamed. "Not yet but they will be.
I'm working on it now that my divorce is
final. She is destined to become the next
Mrs. Johnny Rush."

York held his tongue from saying that
would probably come as a surprise to Danielle. One of his men had followed Danielle
and Felder to their lover's hideaway on the
beach last night. And from the man's report,
he had seen enough to let him know the
two were involved, and it wasn't all Felder's
doing as Johnny assumed.

"Where is Ms. Simone anyway?" York
asked, glancing around.

"She overslept. She had a bad migraine

yesterday and went to bed early last night."

Like hell she did, York almost said.

"She gets to sleep in because her scene isn't getting filmed today," Johnny added.

York didn't say anything; he just nodded. He'd heard of romantic entanglements on movie sets but he figured the one between the leading man, the leading lady and Damien Felder was a bit outrageous.

"Are you sure you don't need me to walk you to your room?"

Darcy glanced up at Damien as they stood in the lobby of her hotel. He'd spent most of the day with her, as well as the evening, going to dinner and a club, but now it was late, close to midnight. She had enjoyed herself but if walking her up to her room meant he assumed he would be staying the night then she rather he didn't. "I'm positive."

"All right then. Can I see you again tomorrow?"

She figured she shouldn't let him dominate her vacation, but she'd had a good time with him. He hadn't tried coming on to her and actually seemed to enjoy her company, as well. "I've made plans to have a day of beauty tomorrow. Most of my time will be spent at the spa and then later the hotel is throwing another party. You can come as my guest if you'd like."

He shook his head. "No, I need to fly to Miami tomorrow night for a couple of days since we won't be filming over the weekend. Can I contact you when I return?"

She saw no reason why he couldn't. "Sure, just call the hotel and ask for me. They will connect you to my room."

"All right, no problem."

If he was bothered about her not giving him her contact information, he wasn't showing it. "And thanks for the tote bag," she said. "I've been doing a lot of shopping, and I intend to fill it up with all sorts of goodies."

He smiled. "No problem. I thought you'd like it since it promotes the movie and will be a memento of your day spent on the set."

"Yes, it will be. Good night, Damien, and thanks again for a wonderful day and evening."

"You're welcome." He then leaned over and placed a kiss on her cheek. "I hope to see you when I return. Not that you need one, but do enjoy your day of beauty tomorrow."

"Thanks for the compliment, and I will."

She turned to head toward the bank of elevators when she felt heat in her midsection. She wasn't surprised when she glanced to her right and saw York sitting at one of the restaurant's tables that gave him a good view of the lobby. Their gazes met, and the penetrating dark eyes staring at her made her increase her pace as she moved toward the elevator. Why did his look have such a mesmerizing effect on her? Even before last night, his stare could get next to her, and after last night, the effect was even worse.

She couldn't help noticing he was frowning, and the frown was so deep she could see the fierce lines of displeasure slashing between the darkness of his eyes. Darcy set her jaw, not caring one iota that he was probably pissed with her for not staying away from Damien.

She stepped on the elevator, and when she turned around, she saw he'd left the restaurant and was heading toward the revolving doors, the same ones Damien had left through moments ago. As she watched him cross the lobby, she couldn't help but think that York Ellis was undoubtedly six feet plus of heart-stopping masculinity. She thought he was an awesome sight last night in a tux, but tonight in a pair of jeans and a pullover shirt, he looked hot.

The elevator door closed, and she backed up against the wall to give others room.

There was no use wishing last night had never happened, because it had, and as much as she wished otherwise, she had no regrets.

Subconsciously, she took her tongue and ran it across her bottom lip when she remembered the searing kiss they'd shared. She wasn't surprised that York was a good kisser and was convinced she could still taste him on her tongue.

You have it bad, girl. You shouldn't go two years without sex again. She couldn't help laughing out loud at that thought. She quickly wiped the amusement off her face when others in the elevator turned to stare at her as if she had a few screws loose.

Hell, maybe she did, because at that moment she knew if given the chance, she would definitely do York again.

CHAPTER 5

Darcy hadn't expected to go all out when she'd arrived at the spa that morning, but a few hours later, she was walking out of the place feeling like a brand-new woman. She was definitely more at peace with herself for the time being. In addition to the body massage, she had waded in the serenity fountains, spent time walking through the private herbal gardens and indulged in a mineral bath. It had been a peaceful interlude, an emotional escape and a chance to let her mind just relax and unwind.

She had needed the peaceful diversion since she had spent the majority of the night tossing between the sheets while memories of what she'd shared with York the previous night racked her body. It was one of those times that Bruce would have probably come in handy. But after York, she was convinced she was putting Bruce in permanent retirement.

She hadn't gotten much sleep as memories washed through her, making her body tense, irritable and in a need that could get satisfied only one way and with only one man. She was totally convinced that no other man would be able to make her body hum the way York had.

She glanced at her watch as she entered her hotel room. More than half of the day had passed by already. She felt another presence the moment she entered her hotel room. She glanced around and nearly dropped the shopping bag filled with items she'd purchased at the spa. York was sitting on her sofa as if he had every right to be there waiting on her return.

She closed the door and glared at him. "How did you get in here?"

He smiled. "I have my ways."

She placed her bags on the table. "Breaking and entering now, York?"

"A man has to do what a man has to do."

She crossed her arms over her chest. "Meaning?"

"I came to check on you."

She watched as he rose to his feet, appreciating the way his entire body moved with charismatic precision, fluidity and an agility that not only held her attention but was dousing her with an arousing effect of sensations. He was wearing a pair of khakis and an island shirt. He looked laid-back, too sinfully sexy for his good — as well as for hers.

Knowing she needed to keep their conversation on a straight and narrow path, she asked, "Why would you need to check on me? You saw Damien return me to the hotel last night. And I saw you follow him, so don't pretend that you didn't."

He shrugged as he placed his hands in his pockets. "Why would I pretend? I told you my reason for being here in Jamaica."

Yes, he had. "But why are you inside my hotel room? Why couldn't you call or sit in the lobby and wait for me there?"

He shrugged. "I don't have your phone number, and why sit in a lobby when I can have a comfortable spot in here?"

Her frown deepened. "You could have contacted me through the hotel's operator."

"I did. I called your room several times, but you didn't answer."

"I spent most of the day at the spa. And you've got a lot of nerve being here. What if I'd brought someone back with me?"

She saw a tick in his jaw when he responded. "Then I guess it would not have been his lucky day."

She felt swamped with varying emotions

at the subtle threat she'd heard in his voice. She fought them off by refusing to believe her having a fling with another man meant anything to him other than the typical male possession. They make love to you and thought they owned you. But she knew of York's reputation with women. He probably wouldn't know how to be possessive of one.

"I'm going to ask you one more time, York. Why are you in my hotel room?"

"I told you," he said, sinking back down on the sofa. "I wanted to make sure you were okay. Evidently you didn't take my warning about Felder at face value. Why are you still seeing him?"

She crossed her arms over her chest. "Because I want to. He hasn't done anything to me, and I enjoy his company."

She then rubbed a frustrated hand down her face. "Look, York, I understand you have a job to do, which is why I didn't give anything away yesterday while we were on set. I pretended we didn't already know each other. You placed me in an awkward position."

"No, I didn't. You placed yourself in an awkward position by being with Felder in the first place."

Darcy felt a headache coming on and decided she needed for York to leave. They weren't getting anywhere. "No need to rehash anything, York. We don't think the same way about things."

"We seemed to be in accord the other night."

She glared at him. "A real gentleman wouldn't bring that up."

He chuckled, but she could tell the amusement on his face was forced. "And who said I was a gentleman?"

Her chin firmed. "Sorry, my mistake."

She licked her lips to keep her teeth from grinding. She just didn't get it. He was right. In bed, they were of one mind, their dislike of each other tossed to the wayside as they concentrated on something else entirely. Something hot and simmering. Pleasure of the most intense kind. However, out of bed they were constantly at each other's throats, bickering, biting each other's heads off.

"Don't you think we should consider a truce?" he asked.

"Why?"

"So we could try and get along."

"We get along as much as we need to," she said, waving off his words. "What I think we should do while we're in Jamaica is put distance between us. This island is big enough for the both of us so our paths shouldn't cross too much."

"Distance won't work now. Problem with that, Darcy, is that I've made love to you."

She looked at him confused. "What does that have to do with anything? I'm sure you've made love to a lot of women over the years."

"But I particularly enjoyed making love to you."

She didn't want to admit that she had definitely enjoyed making love with him as well. But she didn't intend to lose any sleep over it. She drew in a deep breath. Who was she fooling? She had lost sleep over it. Last night she had lain awake in a bad way. She had needed him. She had yearned to be touched the same way and in the same places he had touched her the night before.

"I'm glad you enjoyed our romp between the sheets, York, but we need to move past that. When I left New York to come here, you weren't even on my mind. And I'm sure I wasn't on yours. People have flings all the time with no lasting effects."

"That might be true, but I refuse to believe I'm not on your mind right now or that you don't want me again."

She was so taken back by his direct assertion that she was left momentarily stunned. He was right on both accounts, but she would never admit to it. "You're wrong."

She then watched him ease off the sofa. Seeing him do so was a total turn-on once again. She was so filled with sexual awareness of him that she knew he had to know it. He began walking toward her, and her gaze tracked his every movement. No matter what kind of clothes he wore he was striking, and he had the ability to stir emotions deep inside of her. She considered backing up, running for cover but decided to hold her ground.

"I can prove that I'm right and you know it," he said when he came to a stop in front of her. "You want me to prove it?"

No, she didn't want him to prove it because he would prove her wrong. She figured the best thing to do was to stay on a topic that would keep them at odds with each other. "You don't like Damien," she said.

If the change of subject seemed odd, he didn't let on. "No, I don't like him," he said easily in a hardened voice.

"Why, York? Because he's showing interest in me?"

York drew in a deep breath while tossing Darcy's question around in his head. In a way, she was right but then in a way she was wrong. He decided to be honest with her. "I had reason to suspect Felder of wrongdoing even before seeing the two of you together. But then I will admit that I don't like the interest he's showing in you or the interest you're returning, especially after our time together the other night."

"It was a one-night stand, York. Don't try to make it into more than it was because jealousy doesn't become you."

He had news for her. It was already more than that, and evidently jealousy *did* become him, although he wished otherwise. And he couldn't understand why it mattered to him. He of all people had never been possessive where lovers were concerned. He enjoyed women and had no problem moving on when boredom set in. But he had a feeling Darcy was a woman a man wouldn't get bored with easily.

He hadn't been able to sleep last night for thinking of her, wanting her. And it hadn't helped matters that he'd followed Felder after he'd left her only to see him meet up with Danielle Simone. York was still trying to figure out that angle. If Felder was so into the leading lady then why was he spending as much time as he could with Darcy? And if Rush was so into Danielle, why hadn't he figured out that something more was going on between her and Felder?

After the accusation Darcy had just thrown at him — that he disliked Felder because he was jealous — she wouldn't believe him if he told her the man was probably just using her as a decoy for some unscrupulous purpose. He might as well keep his mouth shut on the subject until he could prove his theory.

In the meantime, there was a subject he wanted to bring up and decided just to come out and ask. "Are you on the Pill or any other type of birth control?" He knew it was crazy but he had lowered his voice, as if there was someone else in the room besides them.

York could tell from her expression that she was surprised not only with the swift change in subject but also with what he'd asked. "Why do you want to know?"

"Because of the other night." The memories were etched in his mind and with her standing there in a cute sundress that showed what a gorgeous pair of legs she had, he could recall the feel of those same legs wrapped around him.

His gaze raked over her, and he couldn't help but appreciate her feminine curves, small waist and firm and full breasts. The fact that she was a looker wasn't helping matters — or the fact that he'd seen her naked.

Seeing the way he was checking her out made her gaze drill into his. "And if I remember correctly . . . and I do . . . you wore a condom each time. I hope you're not about to break the news to me that they were defective or something."

He shook his head. "No, that's not it."

"Then what is it, York?"

He wished she wouldn't ask so many questions. It would really help matters if she just told him what he wanted to know. "I wasn't as careful as I usually am with the condoms," he finally said.

She tilted her head at an angle that pinned him to the spot. "Yes, I happened to notice, but I was enjoying myself too much to call it to your attention."

He laughed. The woman never ceased to amaze him. She said just what she thought or felt.

"I'm glad you find me amusing, York."

"Only when you say whatever the hell you feel like saying," he said.

She shrugged. "And that's all the time. I do the professional thing at work but when I'm out among friends — or those who might not be friends — I am the real me. What you see is what you get. Now to answer your question . . . yes, I'm on some sort of birth control but it's not the Pill. So you're safe this time, and I want to think you're also healthy because I am."

"Yes, I am."

"Good, then there's nothing you need to worry about. I came to Jamaica to relax, read and romp. Since sex was on the list, I definitely came prepared."

She then glanced at her watch. "Don't you have somewhere to go?"

"No. So what about that truce?" he asked her, taking a step closer.

Darcy tried not to notice his fascinatingly sexy mouth, a mouth that had nearly driven her insane two nights ago. She wished she didn't have to think about that now but found she couldn't help herself. "You think a truce will work with us?"

A slow smile touched his lips. "It wouldn't hurt."

She wasn't too convinced of that. When she'd left New York, she'd made plans, had such big ideas of how she wanted her three weeks of vacation to start and end. She'd intended to kick up her legs and have some fun. Well, she'd certainly kicked up her legs, right his way. And he hadn't wasted any time getting between them. "I wouldn't want you to get any ideas."

He chuckled. "About what?"

"What a truce between us means. I didn't come here to have an affair with you."

He flashed her another smile, one that made her body shiver inside. "But you came here intending to have an affair with somebody, right?"

"Yes."

"Then it might as well be me since we've already gotten off to a good start where sex is concerned." He held out his hand. "So, can we agree on a truce? Even if we decide to take sex off the table and never sleep together again?"

She looked at his outstretched hand and asked, "Will you stop accusing Damien of things you're not certain that he's done?"

He frowned. "Why do you keep defending him?"

"And why are you so convinced he's guilty?"

He didn't reply for a moment and then said, "May I suggest we leave Damien out of this for now? This is between me and you."

She narrowed her gaze. "Fine. For now," she said finally taking his hand. The moment she did so she knew it had been a mistake to agree to a truce with him. Stealing a look at him from beneath her lashes, she saw the smoldering look in his gaze.

She knew she should heed the warning bells that suddenly went off in her head, but she didn't have the strength to do so. The man had the ability to blur the line between reason and desire. She pulled her hand from his when it seemed he was in no hurry to release it.

"Have dinner with me tonight, Darcy."

She lifted a brow. "Dinner? What if we're seen together? Would you want that?"

York responded to Darcy's question with a shake of his head. No, he shouldn't want it but he did. And she had openly admitted she'd come to Jamaica for relaxation, reading and sex. Was Felder someone she'd placed on her to-do list? If that was the case then she could scratch him off. He intended to be the only man she made love to while on the island. A part of him knew that sounded crazy. They'd made love that one time, and it didn't give him any right to possess her. But he couldn't help it for some reason.

He was satisfied with the fact that Felder had caught a plane off the island for a few days, and coincidentally, Danielle Simone had left the island as well. He had men tailing them both, and he wouldn't be surprised to receive a call saying they were together somewhere. He couldn't help wonder where that left good old Johnny-boy. What lie had Danielle told him so he wouldn't suspect anything? And why was Darcy being pulled into their little game? What role did they intend for her to play?

"Since filming has stopped for the weekend the majority of the cast and crew have scattered with plans to return on Monday," he said. "But even if they were here, it wouldn't matter to me if we were seen together. But if it makes you feel better, I know just the place to ensure our privacy."

She shrugged beautiful shoulders. "Doesn't matter to me."

He stared at her. Today her skin appeared smoother than before, and the scent emitting from her skin was different from those other times. The fragrance was just as seductive but reminded him of a flower garden. "You sure? There's still that chance that no matter where we go, we might still be seen by someone. So, if you're so into Felder that it would matter if he finds out we were seen together, then say so. I know some women get all excited by those Hollywood types."

He could tell by the tightening of her lips and the flash that appeared in her eyes that she hadn't liked what he'd said. "I'm not one of them. I only spent yesterday with him, and he seems to be a nice guy. I think you're wrong about him, York."

He rolled his eyes. "Just remember there are a lot of nice guys sitting in jail right now, Darcy."

He checked his watch. "What about if I come back around six?"

For a moment, he thought she wouldn't agree, and then she said, "That's fine. I'll be ready."

"And wear something with an accent on having fun. I plan to take you for a walk on the beach later," he said, dragging in a deep breath as he headed for the door. He needed to get out of there now. It wouldn't take much to pull her into his arms for a repeat of what they'd shared two nights ago.

They would make love again. He was certain of it. That night she had been simply amazing, had met him on every level and then in a surprising move, she had ridden him, given him an orgasm that still made his body tremble just thinking about it. Afterward he had been weak, wrung out and exhausted. And then she had proceeded to arouse him all over again.

When he reached her door, he turned unexpectedly, and the guilty look on her face let him know she had been checking him out from behind. The gaze now looking at him was hot. He could easily change their plans and stay in — order room service, then spend a night between the sheets. They could take turns riding each other like they'd done the other night.

A predatory and primitive urge eased up his spine. He felt great satisfaction in knowing she wanted him as much as he wanted her. "I'll see you at six."

Then he opened the door and walked out.

CHAPTER 6

They were just going to dinner and taking a walk on the beach later, Darcy said, looking at herself in the bathroom's full-length mirror. No biggie. It meant nothing.

First of all, York wasn't her type. But she would have to admit he had been the best lover she'd ever had. With him, there were no limitations. He was willing to try just about anything, and she'd had a lot of ideas. When you read as many romance novels as she had over the years, you were bound to have a few unique positions stored up in your brain.

She left her bedroom and entered the living room area. York had said he would return at six, and it was a few minutes to that time. She was dressed, so with nothing else to do, she began pacing the floor, feeling hot and restless.

Another first when it came to York. She would have to give him credit as being the first man she'd dated that not only made her aware of her power as a woman but encouraged her to flaunt it, to wrap herself up in her femininity in a way she'd never done before.

Harold had been a total jerk, she could see that now. In the early days, all she'd wanted to do was to please him, both in and out of the bedroom. But he was never satisfied.

When his job began going bad, he wanted to blame his problems on her since she was happy at her job.

Then after he'd gotten laid off he resented that she was working. That was when the abuse began and when the love and respect she'd thought she had for him went plummeting down the toilet. It was then she'd vowed never to be ruled by another man. They were just heartbreak waiting to happen, and she'd learned her lesson. From what she'd heard, York was just as commitment phobic as she was — smart man.

But the one thing she couldn't forget, although she'd tried, was that they'd made love. He wasn't the first man she'd made love to since her divorce, but she had even put affairs on the back burner. In fact, she'd begun to wonder why she'd even bothered getting those injections for birth control

120

when there hadn't been any real action going down in that neck of the woods. But
York had reminded her of why it was always
important to be prepared for the unex-
pected.

She hadn't expected to make love to him
that night. Nor had she expected him to get
so carried away he would get careless. The
thought of having some man's child would
cross her mind every so often, but she
would push it way to the back. She loved
kids and wanted some of her own one day.
But she knew since she didn't plan to ever
marry again that she would venture into the
life of a single mother.

The knock on the door made her breath
catch in her throat knowing York was standing on the other side. Not surprisingly, he
was right on time. She looked down at
herself. He'd suggested she wear something
for fun; she felt the short tropical-print dress
did the trick. It was one she'd purchased on
one of her infamous shopping sprees. This
was her first time wearing it, and she
couldn't wait to see York's reaction to it.

Her insides were churning when she
opened the door and saw him standing
there. The way his gaze roamed over her
from head to toe made her smile at the look
of male appreciation in the dark depths of

his eyes. She had gotten the reaction she'd wanted and had hoped for.

"Hello, York, you're right on time. It will only take me a second to grab my purse."

She walked over to the table knowing his gaze was following her every step. Usually she didn't wear her dresses this short, but when she'd seen it on a mannequin while shopping with Ellie one day during her best friend's New York visit, El had convinced her it would look even better on her. And from the way York kept looking at her she had a feeling it did. She heard the door close behind him and knew he'd stepped over the threshold to come into the hotel room.

She turned and saw the deep frown on his face. "Is anything wrong?"

He placed his hands in the pockets of his slacks. "I suggested you wear something for fun. Not something to keep me aroused the rest of the evening."

She tossed her head, sending a mass of hair around her shoulders. She couldn't help the smile that touched her lips. "Poor baby. You'll survive. In fact, I'll make sure that you do." She liked the fact that he spoke his mind just like she spoke hers.

She placed the straps of her purse on her shoulder. "I'm ready."

She'd made the statement, but neither of

them made an attempt to move. They just stood there staring at each other. Then he spoke. "Don't think that I don't know what you're up to, Darcy."

She threw him an innocent look. "I have no idea what you're talking about." She then smiled smugly. "But then, maybe I do."

He took his hands out of his pockets and placed them across his chest. "You play with fire, and you're liable to get burned."

She gave him a thoughtful look. She'd already encountered his fire and knew how hot he was capable of getting things. And as long as he was the one doing the burning she wouldn't back down. "Fire doesn't scare me, York."

He shook his head and chuckled. "Maybe it should. Come on, let's get out of here."

She led the way out of the hotel room, figuring he was still enjoying the backside view. "So where are you taking me?" she asked when they reached the elevator.

He smiled down at her. "You'll see."

York was glad there were others on the elevator with them or else he would have been tempted to take her right then and there. Every single cell in his body had to be aroused right now, thanks to the sexiest minidress a woman could wear. And she definitely had the body for it. He could just imagine other men checking her out in this outfit and felt pressure at the top of his head just thinking about it. Now he was glad he'd made the decision to take her to a place where it would be just the two of them.

His lips thinned when he recalled that he had run into Johnny Rush on the way up to Darcy's room. He knew for a fact the man was staying at a hotel a few miles away, so who had he been visiting here at this hotel? If he'd expected to drop in on Danielle Simone, then he'd discovered she was long gone, since Danielle and Felder were together in Miami.

"You've gotten quiet on me, York."

He glanced down at Darcy as he led her through the hotel's glass doors. Just as he'd figured, they'd gotten plenty of attention walking across the lobby. Men had literally stopped what they were doing to stare at her. And he had seen the look of envy in their eyes when they'd gazed at him walking by her side.

"Um, I'm thinking about all the heat you and I seem to stir whenever we're together."

Instead of making a comment, she arched her brows. There was no need for him to elaborate. He was certain that she understood what he was talking about. Even now

124

he was convinced he could still taste the most recent kiss they'd shared.

He studied her underneath his lashes and thought now the same thing he'd thought when he first saw her that day two years ago. She was a whirlwind and could probably have a man falling for her without much effort on her part. You couldn't help but be drawn to her. And now he wanted to get to know the real Darcy Owens — uncensored, up close and personal. He knew she figured since they had slept together that should be the end of it, and maybe under normal circumstances that would be. But as far as he was concerned, the circumstances weren't normal. They shared the same close friends, yet there was a lot about her that he didn't know. He wanted to get to know her better. He *intended* to get to know her better.

It didn't take long for the valet to bring his rental car to him. Watching her get in the car and ease down on the leather seats in that dress was worth the last few sleepless nights he'd endured thinking about her. She definitely had nice thighs, shapely and perfect for her legs. He wanted her. He had been convinced that a strong-willed woman turned him off, but the one sitting in the car beside him in that short dress turned him on big-time.

"Penny for your thoughts," she said when they had driven away from the hotel.

He hadn't said anything for a while, trying to get his thoughts and his libido under control. He glanced over at her and decided to be honest. "I was thinking about making love to you again. I want you."

He did no more than steal a quick glance at her expression before turning his gaze back to the road. He'd seen what he had wanted to see. A mirror image of the desire he felt was reflected in her shocked gaze. He was beginning to understand just how to handle Darcy. She didn't need a man who sugarcoated anything but a man who could dish it out just like she could. She spoke her mind and appreciated a man who did the same.

She was different from the women he usually dated, those who preferred being told what they wanted to hear. And he had no trouble obliging them if he got what he wanted in the end. With Darcy, there was no need to play games or talk in circles. He liked that.

When he braked the car to a stop at the traffic light, on impulse he reached over and traced his fingertips along her thigh, liking the way her skin felt there — soft and smooth. He couldn't help but remember how it felt riding those same thighs and how those thighs had also ridden him.

He glanced over at her and saw fire flaring in the depths of her eyes. It was fire he'd generated, fire he intended to stir into a huge flame, fire he intended to extinguish in his own special way. He returned his hand back to the steering wheel when the traffic light changed.

"What's your sign, York?"

He chuckled. Now she was going to try and figure him out. He really wasn't a complicated sort of guy. He was just a horny one at the moment, thanks to her. He answered merely to amuse her. "Scorpio."

Now it was her turn to chuckle before saying, "I figured as much."

He wasn't into that astrology stuff but was curious as to how she'd figured it. "You need to expound on that."

"No problem." And then she said, "Scorpios are very passionate beings. They crave physical contact. In other words, they love sex."

He wouldn't go so far as to say he loved sex, but he certainly enjoyed it. "And how would you know that?"

"Because I'm a Scorpio."

If her words were meant to make him get

hard, they succeeded. The erection already there got even harder, bigger. The thought that she liked sex made him throb. He should have figured that much from when they'd made love. There had been something else about that night that stayed with him. He could tell that it had been a long time since she'd made love to a man. Her body was tight. And if that hadn't been enough to give something away, he couldn't forget that several times in the course of their lovemaking she'd let it slip that it had been a long time for her, which was why she thought she was being so greedy. If she loved sex so much, why had she gone without?

He decided to ask her. "Then why did you go without it for a long time?"

She looked at him as if wondering how he'd known and he said, "That night, you let it slip that it had been a long time for you."

How much time passed before she answered he wasn't sure, but he was certain he'd been holding his breath for her response. Finally she said, "I hadn't meant to tell you that, but I guess I sort of got caught up in the moment."

He smiled remembering. "You did. So did I," he said, not ashamed to admit it.

He could feel the constant thump of his heart in his chest when she said, "Yes, it had been a long time for me."

"Why?"

He thought she would tell him it wasn't any of his business. She certainly had every right to do so. Instead she surprised him by saying, "I decided to take a two-year hiatus. I was starting a new job and needed to stay focused on something other than male body parts. Besides, I had gotten out of one hell of a marriage and refused to even consider getting into a serious relationship."

He brought the car to another stop. He'd heard from Uriel that her ex-husband had been a jerk. "If you like sex so much, how did you survive going without it?"

She shrugged delicate-looking shoulders beneath her spaghetti straps. "I had my ways of keeping myself entertained."

He quickly caught on to what she'd meant. What a pity. A woman with profound needs should not have had to settle for a substitute.

"We might as well clear things up about something else while we're in a talkative mood, York."

He glanced over at her. "About what?"

"That day we met at Uriel and Ellie's wedding and you tried coming on to me and

I was a smart-ass and all but told you to go screw yourself."

He could clearly recall that day, and that's not all she'd said. "Yes? What about it?"

"I was in a bad mood. I had just received a call from my ex that he intended to make my life miserable by moving to New York just to aggravate the hell out of me."

"So you took it out on me?"

"I would have taken it out on anyone with a penis, and you just happened to be the first man who approached me after that phone call."

He remembered she had left the wedding rehearsal for a short while, and when she'd returned he had hightailed it over to her to see if she wanted to go out with him later that night. Her words had set his face on fire, and he'd walked off intending to never have anything to do with her again.

"I took it out on you, and I apologize."

Her apology was two years in coming, but there was no need for either of them to hold a grudge forever. But still . . . "Why are you apologizing now, Darcy?"

"Because I think I should. Okay, I admit I should have done so long ago, but every time I ran into you at one of Ellie's functions, you would avoid me like I had a disease or something and it sort of pissed me off."

He frowned as he stared over at her. "And after what you said to me, you really expected me not to avoid you? You threatened to all but castrate me if I got in your face again."

"Okay, I remember all that, and I'm sorry. Do you accept my apology?"

He drew in a deep breath. It would be silly if he didn't, especially since he knew for a fact she wouldn't harm that particular body part. She'd held it in her hand, had taken it in her mouth. The memory of her doing both was increasing his arousal. "Yes, I accept your apology. It's in the past, so let's leave it there. We've moved beyond that now, haven't we?"

"Yes. Ellie will be glad to hear we're no longer enemies. That bothered her," she said.

He decided not to say that their less than friendly attitude never bothered Uriel. It had taken a while for Darcy to grow on him, as well. It had something to do with a prank Darcy had gotten Ellie to play on Uriel when the two women were in their teens. It had taken Uriel a long time to get over it.

"You and Ellie been best friends a long time?" he asked her.

"Almost forever. She's the sister I never

had, and since she was an only child, I got to go a lot of places with her, like to Cavanaugh Lake for the summers."

Since he was godbrother to Uriel, whose parents also owned a place at Cavanaugh Lake, he spent a lot of his summers there as well. He could remember Ellie and her annoying little friend but hadn't known until Ellie and Uriel's wedding that Darcy had been that annoying friend. She had grown into a beautiful woman — not that she'd been an ugly kid or anything but just one not all that noticeable. Besides, she'd been five years younger, and he'd never paid her much attention. Now he did.

"So you're not telling me where we're going?" she asked, glancing over at him.

He smiled. "Not yet. We'll be there in a minute. Just relax. You have nothing to worry about."

Darcy wasn't too sure of that. Just sharing a car with York was pure torture. The man was too virile. When he made such blatant statements as he'd done earlier, he made her remember everything about the night they'd made love.

Being coy was not a part of her makeup, and it seemed it wasn't a part of his either. She liked that, and she hated to admit it —

since they had avoided each other for so long — that she kind of liked him, too. He was a Scorpio; so was she. According to their signs when it came to compatibility, a Scorpio and Scorpio match was rated high, the same when it came to sex between a Scorpio and a Scorpio. So it seemed they had that in the bag. After the other night, she had no reason not to believe it. But the ratings weren't so high when it came to communication between two Scorpios. She wondered why. She enjoyed discussing things with York, at least when they stayed away from controversial subjects like Damien Felder. York had his own opinions about the man, and she had hers.

She was glad she'd apologized for her behavior two years ago. Ellie had kept telling her that she should, and like she'd told him, she had tried. But he hadn't given her the opportunity. Even that night when he'd shown up at her place because Ellie had convinced him to come, he had come arguing about it, which set her off again.

"How do you like your job as a city planner?"

She looked over at him. "I like it on those days politics aren't involved." On the days it was, she wanted to quit and do something else. But her job paid her well even with the headaches. And she did enjoy living in New York, especially when the weather was nice. There were so many things to see and do.

"So, did your ex follow you to New York?" he asked her.

"Yes, and he tried making my life a living hell for a couple of months. I ended up getting a restraining order on him. That's the reason Ellie had you rush over to my place that night. She was convinced my intruder was Harold."

Over the next few minutes she engaged in conversation with him and found herself telling him the reason she had gotten a divorce.

She also told him about her job and that she hadn't taken a lot of time off for the two years she'd worked as a city planner and that in addition to much needed R & R, she'd also had wanted to escape the cold weather in New York for a while.

And just the opposite, he told her how much he enjoyed New York winters and that he was missing the snowstorm passing through even now. As they talked, it dawned on her just how laid-back he was once you got to know him. She was enjoying the conversation. He was arrogant, true enough, but there was something about his arrogance that she found as a total turn-on at times.

And she couldn't dismiss the fact that being with him did something to her, gave her an adrenaline rush like she'd never experienced before. Especially when he was so up front and candid about certain things. She had a feeling how he intended the evening to end. He'd all but spelled it out to her. The thought that he pretty much had sexual ideas that included her didn't bother her in the least. In fact, if truth be told, she was still in awe of their lovemaking the other night. Although at the time she'd figured it was one and done, it still had lingering effects on her.

She couldn't look at her naked body in the mirror without remembering how he'd licked every single inch of it. And her nipples would strain against her top when she recalled how he had sucked the dark pebbles into his mouth and feasted on them. Even now, the memory of his head between her legs had heat rushing all through her.

"What are your plans for the holidays, Darcy?"

She glanced over at him, wondering why he'd want to know and then quickly figured he'd asked for conversational purposes only.

"When I leave here, instead of flying back to New York, I'm headed to Minnesota to spend Christmas with my parents and brothers. I've timed it to be with them Christmas Eve and Christmas Day. That's the most I can take of the harsh, cold Minnesota weather. Then on the day after Christmas I'm heading to Cavanaugh Lake to help Ellie with her New Year's Eve bash. She's planning a masquerade party this year."

"That should be interesting and a lot of fun."

She thought so as well and looked forward to the event.

As the car continued to move through the streets of Jamaica, she glanced out the window to take in the sights they passed. They were on the grander side of the island, where the wealthy resided, which was evident by the spacious homes they passed. She knew the houses were owned by wealthy Americans and Europeans who wanted to get away to the tropical island whenever they could. Cheyenne Steele Westmoreland and Vanessa Steele Cody, along with their husbands, owned beautiful homes in this part of the island as well. The two women were first cousins to Donovan Steele, a close friend of Uriel's. She had met most of the

Steele family through Ellie at family functions and gatherings.

It had turned dark, and the lights that lined the streets seemed to shimmer across the water. When York turned off the main road and onto a street lined with palm trees on both sides, she studied the homes they passed. Huge, magnificent and beautiful were just a few words she could use to describe them. And when he pulled into the driveway of one such home, she turned and glanced over at him questioningly.

He smiled. "This is where we'll be spending the evening. I plan to treat you to my own brand of an island feast."

She glanced back at the house and then back at him. "And the owner has no problem with you doing that?" she asked, trying to downplay her excitement at the thought that he wanted to prepare a meal for her.

He chuckled. "Trust me, he won't mind since I know him well."

"Do you?"

"Yes. I own the place. And I want to welcome you, Darcy Owens, to my summer home in Jamaica."

CHAPTER 7

York leaned back against the closed door and watched as Darcy moved around his living room. It was as if she was fascinated by each and every thing she saw, whether it was the furniture, the paintings on the wall or the large potted plants he had strategically arranged to get the optimum amount of sun. Then there was the sea view from every window.

He had bought the home when it had been in foreclosure and never regretted doing so. It was his haven, his escape when he'd found himself working too hard and needing playtime. He liked spending time on the water and owned a Jet Ski that he enjoyed taking out every chance he got.

"This place is beautiful, York, and the view of the ocean is simply breathtaking."

"Thanks." He smiled, pleased with her assessment of his home. He was a man who really never cared what others thought of his possessions, but knowing she liked this place filled him with something he'd never felt before. It was then that he realized he had never brought a woman here. Usually his time spent at this place was what he considered as "me" time — his time alone to unwind and enjoy the beach that was literally in his backyard.

He studied her as she continued to look out one of his floor-to-ceiling windows and thought she was breathtaking, as well. That short dress had practically undone him the moment he'd seen her in it. She was the only woman that could get him wound up to this point, where he was filled with a simmering need that was hard to keep in check. And it didn't help matters to know he'd already sampled her, already knew her taste and scent. Knew how it felt to ride her.

She turned and caught him staring but didn't seem surprised. He had a feeling she was aware of every move he made. He wondered if she was privy to his thoughts as well. If she was, then she knew those thoughts were salacious, indecent at best, highly X-rated. Even now he was wondering what was or wasn't under her dress.

He drew in a long breath when their gazes held, and the silence between them was becoming noticeably long. It wouldn't take much to cross the room, lift that short dress and take her just where she stood.

It was she who finally broke the silence by asking, "How long have you owned the house?"

"A few years. I always wanted a place on the island, and when I heard about it I couldn't pass up the chance to get it. It's my escape from reality. I've been a beach bum here a time or two."

"Why are you staying at the hotel when you have this place?"

He moved away from the door. "I'm on the island working, and I need to be in the thick of things."

"Oh."

He knew his words reminded her of his allegations about Felder. She tilted back her head, stared at him and asked, "Why are you so hell-bent on Damien Felder being guilty?"

"And why are you so hell-bent that he's innocent?"

He could feel a confrontation coming on, and he could deal with that. A verbal sparring with her was always refreshing. But what he didn't like was the thought that they would be arguing about another man — a man who when he wasn't with her was sleeping with another woman. And it was a

woman who another man wanted or assumed he had. If that wasn't a mixed-up affair, he didn't know what was. He didn't
want Darcy to be a part of such foolishness.

"I like giving people the benefit of the
doubt, York."

He rolled his shoulders in a shrug. "That's
a nice gesture, but people aren't always what
they seem to be."

"I know that," she all but snapped and he
had a feeling she wanted to smack him.

"Did Felder make that much of an impression on you, or do you just want to refute
what I say just for the hell of it?" he asked,
regarding her intently.

She smiled, and he thought back to the
first time he had seen her smile . . . although
the smile had not been directed at him. It
had been at Uriel and Ellie's wedding, and
she'd smiled a lot, genuinely happy for her
best friend. And her hazel eyes had sparkled
a lot that night, too.

"You shouldn't be so quick to jump to
conclusions about people, York," she said,
interrupting his thoughts.

"And you think that's what I'm doing?"
he asked.

"Don't you?"

"No. And for you to assume I would
consider a man guilty of wrongdoing just

141

because he's shown an interest in you is unfair to me."

He knew his comment had given her food for thought when she hung her head to study the grain of the wood on his floor. She lifted her head. "You're right, and I owe you another apology."

"Yes, you do."

She frowned. "You don't have to rub it in."

He began slowly walking toward her, and the frown on her face showed no signs of disappearing. In fact, it deepened, and he thought she looked pretty darn sexy when angry. He came to a stop in front of her and said, "I didn't bring you here to argue with you, Darcy."

She tilted her head at an angle to meet his direct gaze. "And why *did* you bring me here?"

He smiled. "To feed you, for starters. You can have a seat here in the living room and enjoy a view of the water, or you can join me in the kitchen to see what else I can do beside nab the bad guys."

He could tell by the light that lit her eyes that the latter suggestion caught her interest. He was proven right when she said, "I'll join you in the kitchen."

■ ■ ■ ■

Darcy sat on a stool at the breakfast bar and sipped a glass of wine as she watched York in action. She was paying attention to how well he handled himself in the kitchen as he went about chopping vegetables to go with the chicken he'd put in the oven to bake.

But her attention went beyond that. For such a tall, well-built guy, he was quick on his feet as he moved around the huge kitchen. It was obvious that he knew his way around the room, which meant he spent a lot of time in it. A man with decent cooking skills was hard to come by these days. And she liked how he could carry on a conversation with her while preparing their food. He liked giving her pointers about how to keep the chicken moist and the easiest way to chop the vegetables so they could retain their nutritional value under heat.

However, what she enjoyed the most was just sitting there and watching him while memories of their one night together continued to consume her. The man was handsome and well built. And his ruggedly handsome features were definitely a plus in her book. He looked good in jeans, and any woman would appreciate the way his muscle shirt covered his broad shoulders. He was definitely eye candy.

She was fairly certain that with his looks and build York could have his pick of women and probably did. Although he'd never brought one to any of the functions Ellie gave, she knew he dated a lot. She'd heard that right after his lover's death he had quit the NYPD and traveled abroad for a year with another one of his godbrothers by the name of Zion Blackstone. Zion had continued living abroad but York had returned to the States and instead of returning to work as a police officer, he had opened his own security firm with money his grandmother had left for him when she'd died. That had been over five years ago, and now his security business was a successful one, and he had nine employees working for him.

"Tell me about some of the cases your company has handled."

He glanced up at her and smiled. "Why? You thinking about changing professions?"

She chuckled. "Um, you never know. Right now, anything would be more appealing than having to deal with the politics of getting things done. Everyone loves New York, but my job is to make sure they continue to love it. Budget cuts haven't helped things."

"I'm sure they haven't." He then began telling her about one of his cases that involved protecting a well-known celebrity from an overzealous fan. "The woman was eventually arrested," he said.

Darcy nodded. She had her favorite celebrities but couldn't for the life of her imagine herself stalking any of them.

"Everything is almost ready. I can give you a tour of the place while we're waiting for the chicken to finish baking."

"Thanks. I'd like that."

York thought that the only thing better than a woman who looked good was one who smelled good as well. And Darcy smelled good. He wasn't sure of what cologne she was wearing tonight, but it was one that made everything inside of him feel primitive and male each time he sniffed it.

She walked beside him as he took her from room to room. It was a big place, but it was cozy enough for him and he made use of every available space. But then he didn't believe in overcrowding. He had hired a private decorator and had been pleased with the results.

As soon as he entered his bedroom and saw his huge bed, he immediately thought of Darcy sharing it with him. And he had a feeling before the night was over, she would. He'd told her on the way here that he wanted her. Nothing had changed. And he'd been aware of how she had been watching him while he'd prepared dinner. Knowing that her eyes had been on him, studying his every move, had made him want her even more.

When they returned to the living room, she sat down on the leather sofa; he sat opposite her on the matching love seat. He watched her cross her legs and clasp her hands together in her lap. The simple gestures turned him on. She had that much of an impact on him without even trying.

And then he watched as she took a sip from her wineglass and remembered just how well she could use that mouth of hers. Suddenly he envisioned Darcy in his bed riding him while he kissed her senseless. He imagined them flipping positions so he could ride her. And just like before, he would ride her hard.

He sat there and listened while she talked, telling him more about her job and then about some of the escapades she and Ellie had gotten into as children. When he asked her about the prank they had once played on Uriel, she told him how she had talked a sixteen-year-old Ellie into kissing Uriel on a dare. Uriel had been in college at the time and hadn't liked it one bit. In fact, it had taken him a while to get over it and his anger had been with Darcy just as much as it had been with Ellie. He could tell by the sparkle in her eyes and the laughter in her voice while she retold the story that she still thought what happened that day had been funny, especially when a furious twenty-one-year-old Uriel had found out he'd been set up by two teenage girls.

York checked his watch before glancing up in time to see her take her last sip of wine. He liked the way the liquid trickled down her throat and remembered how his tongue had licked that part of her. He stood. "Let's get dinner out of the way so we can take a walk on the beach."

She stood as well and returned his smile. "I'm definitely looking forward to that."

Men, Darcy thought, glancing across the table at York, could be unpredictable creatures at times. On the drive over, York had all but hinted he would jump her bones the first chance he got. Yet, she had been here for a couple of hours and he had yet to make a move on her. She wondered if he really did have plans for them to take a walk on the beach.

"You've gotten quiet on me, Darcy."

She chuckled, deciding she wouldn't share what she'd been thinking. "Dinner was delicious," she said, slightly pushing away from the table. And she meant it. He had done an outstanding job.

"Ready to spend some time on the beach?"

So he had been serious. "Sure."

He glanced down at her shoes. "Go ahead and take them off. You're going to love the feel of the sand beneath your feet."

"All right."

She kicked off her sandals and watched as he did the same for his own. She noticed he grabbed a blanket off a shelf before leading her out of his back door. It was dark, and she could hear the sound of the sea roaring through her ears, while the scent of salt water filled her nostrils. He took her hand and they began walking to the beach, which was right in his backyard.

When she'd had thoughts of spending three weeks in Jamaica, her plans included meeting a man with whom she would share a walk on the beach. At the time, she hadn't thought the man would be York.

He'd been right. She liked the feel of the sand beneath her feet, and that combined with the scent of the beach and the knowledge that she had a virile man walking beside her, one whose fingers were entwined with hers, was reminding her of just how much of a woman she was.

It also reminded her of what had happened once already between them and what she looked forward to happening again. Before this trip, she had gone without sex long enough, so wanting to make up for lost time was a strong and healthy urge. Making love to York that night had been like a welcome back to life. She felt good and knew without any doubt that she wanted York again.

"This is a good spot."

They stopped walking, and he released her hand to spread the blanket on the sand. It was dark, but the brightly lit lantern on his back porch provided enough light to see their surroundings. And then there were the stars that dotted the sky overhead and the full moon right in front of them that cast a romantic glow upon where they were. It was like a scene straight out of one of her romance novels. There was nothing better than a romantic night and an ultra-handsome man. A woman couldn't ask for much more.

"That's that," York said, interrupting her

thoughts. She saw he had finished spreading the blanket out and had turned toward her. He was standing about five feet away, yet she was able to feel the moment their gazes connected. Desire immediately began oozing through her bloodstream. Her lips suddenly felt dry, and she automatically ran the tip of her tongue over her bottom lip and was well aware his gaze had followed the movement.

She wanted him. He wanted her. It was all about lust. He knew it, and she knew it, as well. The man had haunted her thoughts since making love to her two nights ago. She had tried convincing herself the reason she'd had gotten so into him the way she had was because he had been her first in two years. But now she knew that excuse wouldn't fly. It was deeper than that. As a lover, he had not only satisfied her yearning but he had also captivated her mind. No other man had been able to do the latter, not even Harold.

She tilted her head as an intense yearning continued to fill her. Refusing to be denied what she wanted, she sauntered toward York, deciding she had no problem making the first move if things called for that. There was a slight breeze in the air that carried moisture to dampen her skin, and the night

air seemed to carry the sound of her foot-
steps in the sand.

There was something about being out on
the beach tonight with York and the way he
was standing there not moving, watching
her and waiting for her to come to him. Her
inner thighs clenched with every step she
took, and she breathed in deeply when she
came to a stop in front of him.

Later, she would wonder why they were
opposites capable of becoming magnets that
could attract each other in such a volatile
way — and why the need to make love to
him on the beach was a *must do* on her list.

He didn't say anything for a long moment.
He just stood there and stared at her, letting his gaze roam up and down her as if he
could see through her clothes. And then,
when she thought she could not take any
more of his blatant perusal or the intense
yearning filling her to capacity, he reached
out and pulled her to him. He pressed her
body close to his, letting her feel just how
hard and erect he was for her. Her breasts,
pressed hard against his chest, began to
throb, and she breathed in his scent at the
same time she felt a tingling sensation
between her thighs.

"I could make love to you out here all
night, Darcy."

His words, spoken in a deep, desire-laced voice, inflamed her mind and she nearly released a groan when she felt the erection pressed against her get even larger. The feel of it sent heat rushing through her, and her breathing became labored. Making love on the beach under the stars with a man had always been a fantasy of hers after reading such a scene in a romance novel. Now here she was with York and a burst of desire, the magnitude of which she'd only ever experienced with him, was taking over her senses.

She studied the gaze staring back at her, saw the need that was as deep as her own. She reached out and pressed her hand to his chest and felt the hard, thumping beat of his heart beneath her palm. How could she feel this immediate desire for him and not for Damien?

She wasn't sure just how much time had elapsed while they stood there, with intense desire building between them by the second. Then, not able to handle the anticipation any longer or the forceful longing, she rose up on her tiptoes, leaned in and took that same tip of her tongue she'd used to moisten her lip earlier and ran it along his jaw. She heard the sound of his heavy breathing in her ear. She heard his moan. She felt the hardness of him swell even more against her belly.

"Will your neighbors see us out here?" she whispered as she continued to use the tip of her tongue to lick underneath his ear. She liked the taste of his skin, hot against her tongue.

"No," he said huskily. "They can't see a thing. The homes on this beach were built to provide ultimate privacy."

"Are you sure?"

"Positive."

Taking his word, she stepped back and began removing her dress. To be honest, even if his neighbors could see anything she was beyond stopping at this point. Modesty was the last thing on her mind. Him getting inside of her and stroking her to a powerful orgasm headed the list right now. The prospect of that happening consumed her thoughts. The breeze whispering in off the water did nothing to cool her heat. It merely intensified it.

She eased her dress up to her waist, and it didn't take long to whip the garment over her head. She hadn't worn a bra, and her thong slid down her legs easily. As the breeze flitted across her naked skin, she knew what this night held for her, and she couldn't downplay her body's excitement or the urges that were taking over her mind and making her want him even more. She was filled with the need for him with every catch of her breath.

York had stood there and watched Darcy strip, and now seeing her without clothes did something to him. He quickly unzipped his jeans and removed them. Then came his briefs and shirt. When he stood before her completely naked, he took the time to sheath a condom over his engorged shaft. His hand nearly trembled with the need for her.

Never had he known a woman quite like her, and in a way, he'd known she would be the one to send his mind in a topsy-turvy. He had hit on her that first time, and when she had rejected his interest, he should have been grateful for her sparing his sanity. Instead he had been resentful. Now he knew it hadn't been meant for them to connect then. But now the field was wide open, and there was no stopping them. It had taken two years for him to accept the intensity of his desire for her, even when he hadn't wanted to crave her to such a degree.

He reached out for her. Instead of lowering her on the blanket, he swept her into his arms and began heading toward the water.

"Where are you taking me, York?"

He glanced down at her and smiled. "You'll see."

And moments later he lowered her naked body into one of those heavyweight vinyl floaters. The inflatable floor cushioned her backside, and he shifted her position to where her legs were spread open. The raft was large enough for more than one person, and he joined her, bracing himself against the side to stare down at her, taking note of the position he'd placed her in, all spread open for him to see. He then took his hand and traced a path up her inner thigh. Then his fingers began inching inside of her, and he studied the emotions that crossed her face when they did.

"You're hot," he said in a deep, husky tone. "You're still tight, and I plan to loosen you up a bit."

"Is that a promise?" she asked, in a whimpering tone.

"Definitely a promise."

And then he shifted positions to straddle her while simultaneously sliding his hands beneath her hips to lift her backside to receive him. His entry inside her was swift, and his heart began thumping hard in his chest when his thrust went to the hilt as he spread her legs farther apart, making them hang off the sides of the raft.

He used his hands to push the raft into the water, and as soon as they were afloat, he began moving in and out of her. This was crazy, but he wanted her this way. He wanted her here. Making love to a woman on a raft in the water had always been a fantasy of his and now he was doing it here with Darcy — only with Darcy.

It was a new float, one he had purchased recently, one that hadn't ever been in the water. Now he was using it for the first time, officially christening it with her. With the water flapping beneath them, every stroke inside of her made his want that much more intense. The low ache in his belly was being appeased with every thrust.

He wanted to make her his.

Why such a thought had even crossed his mind, had lurked its way into his thoughts, he wasn't sure. All he knew at that moment was that he intended to be the only man to ever make love to her in a raft, on the beach or any place else. There would be no Damien Felder in her future. Anyone who knew York was well aware that once he staked a claim about anything that was that. With every lunge into her body, he was doing more than staking a claim; he was declaring possession.

■ ■ ■ ■

Darcy moaned deep within her throat when York's thrust became ever more powerful. She had fantasized about making love on the beach, but doing so in a raft in the water hadn't crossed her mind. And with each breath she was taking, York was driving into her, pushing her over the edge. His thrusts were hard and so intense she figured they would tumble out of the raft and into the water, never to be heard from again. But he managed to handle both her and the raft. He might be keeping the watercraft afloat, but her mind and body were drowning in waters so sensual that she had to pull in deep breaths to survive what he was doing.

What if they ended up in one of his neighbors' backyards or right smack in the middle of the sea? She could see the headlines now. "Man and woman found naked on a raft — bodies can't be pried apart."

That scenario should concern her, but instead she pushed it to the back of her mind. It couldn't compete with the sensations tearing through her. And when York shifted his body slightly and touched an inner part of her that had never been touched before, she screamed. Then an orgasm rammed through her and shook her to the core. The feelings were so intense that he had to grip down on her to keep her body from pushing them both out of the raft and into the water.

He was stroking her into sweet oblivion, and she closed her eyes and threw her head back when she burst into a second orgasm. She moaned his name, and when his mouth captured her to silence the sound, she felt his body buck above her just seconds before he drove even deeper into her.

He released her mouth, and she bit down on her bottom lip to keep from screaming out again. The motion of the water beneath them sent waves of pleasure through her. She opened her eyes and saw he was staring down at her and the sound emitting from between his clenched lips could be considered a growl.

"You're mine, Darcy."

The strong tread of York's voice floated through her mind. She heard his words but couldn't fathom why he'd said them or what he meant by them. She quickly figured he had gotten caught up in the moment and tomorrow he wouldn't even remember them.

As he continued to push her into another orgasm, she knew his virility was unlimited, his desire was primitive and his ability to bring her pleasure was unprecedented. Her breathing got shallow as sensual bliss took over her mind and body. Her heart raced so fast she thought she might faint.

Several pleasure-filled moments later, her body calmed, and when she felt him lift off her she felt an intense sense of loss. She was too afraid to look around, too nervous about where they might have drifted.

"You okay, baby?"

His question made her glance up at him, and she saw the stars were still dotting the sky overhead. At least it was still nighttime. She hadn't been sure how much time had passed. When you were in the throes of extreme sexual pleasure, you were destined to forget about time.

She shifted and moved her legs. If they were out in the middle of the sea, she didn't want her legs hanging over the sides. Sharks could be hungry creatures, and she didn't want to be one's meal.

"Where are we?" she asked him

He smiled. "Out in the water."

She couldn't help returning his smile. "Please tell me we're not near a cruise ship and that you can still see land."

He chuckled, and it was then that she realized just how large the raft was. "No cruise ship on the horizon and yes, we can still see land. I'll have us back to shore in no time."

She felt both relief and excitement upon hearing that. "You sure?"

"Positive."

Believing him, she sat up and let out a deep sigh of relief when she saw they were probably no more than fifty feet from land. He pulled oars — that she noticed for the first time — from the sides of the raft and began using them.

"Need help?" she asked him.

He smiled over at her, his pupils glimmered with sensuality. "No. I got us out here, and I'll get us back. No problem. Besides, I want you to keep all your energy for later."

She took his words as an indication of what was yet to come. He wasn't through with her yet, and she didn't have a problem with any plans his mind was conjuring up. No small surprise there. He could create an intense yearning within her, a hunger, with just a look. She'd thought it before and still thought it now. She'd never met a man quite like York.

As they got closer and closer to land, she could feel the quickened beat of her heart, and as she watched him handle the oars, she saw as well as felt his strength. His broad chest, belly and hips tightened with every push and pull of the oars, and he was still hard and fully erected. She was entranced with the sight before her. His naked body was a total turn-on and knowing what that body had done to her was unforgettable.

She could tell from the way he was looking at her that he was fully aware of just how much he had satisfied her. No doubt even in the moonlight her face was basking with a heated glow that only the pleasures of lovemaking could cause.

She blinked when the raft hit land and then he was out of it to secure it. Then he was reaching for her, carrying her into his arms toward the blanket. Moments later, he was lowering her onto it. By the time she felt the material against her back, York had spread her thighs and was settling between them. He looked down at her and their gazes held. When he entered her, stretching her again, she knew tonight would be one she would remember for a long time.

CHAPTER 8

He was a bachelor undone, York decided as he eased out of bed the next morning. And the woman who had slept beside him all night was responsible. He glanced over at her as he made his way to the bathroom. After making love to her on the blanket several times under the moonlight, he had carried her inside and they had showered together, washing sand from their bodies. Eventually they made love again.

They had tumbled into bed too exhausted to make love in the place where most normal people did, but just like she had christened his raft he had plans for that bed. He figured she would be sleeping a while and after washing his face, brushing his teeth and slipping into a pair of jeans he padded barefoot and bare chested out the room and down the stairs.

He checked his phone and saw he'd missed several calls. One was from Rich, the man he had tailing Felder, and the other two were from Uriel. He quickly called Rich back, and a few moments later the man had brought him up to date. Felder and Danielle Simone were still together, and another interesting fact was that the couple had gotten a visit from someone else, a man not yet identified. But that man was now, too, being tailed as well.

When York ended the call with Rich he called Uriel. "You called?" he asked the moment he heard his godbrother's voice.

"Where the hell are you, Y?"

"I'm in Jamaica working on a case."

"Oh." Then Uriel said, "You probably could care less, but Ellie mentioned that Darcy went to Jamaica on vacation."

"You don't say," he murmured, smiling.

"I do say, so don't be surprised if you run into her."

Evidently Darcy hadn't mentioned to Ellie that she'd seen him on the island, so he wouldn't give anything away. "Thanks for the warning."

"No problem. I called to give you some news."

"What?"

"I got a call from Donovan."

York nodded. Donovan Steele was one of Uriel's closest friends from college. "Yes?"

"He told me that Eli's getting married."

York almost dropped the phone. Eli Steele was one of Donovan's cousins who lived in Phoenix. York and the rest of his godbrothers had gotten to know Eli and his five brothers when they'd traveled as a group to the NASCAR races to support Bronson Scott, Donovan's best friend who was also a mutual friend to everyone.

"He's getting married?" York asked. Eli was the second of the Phoenix Steeles to marry in a year's time. What was surprising was that those Steeles were diehard bachelors who'd vowed never to marry.

"Yes, he's marrying on Christmas Day. Can you believe that?"

York was finding it hard to believe. Earlier that year, Eli's brother Galen had gotten hitched to some woman he'd known less than a month. It wouldn't be such a shocker if Eli and Galen, along with their other brothers, hadn't been known womanizers. For them to settle down with one woman was more than a surprise. It was a downright shock.

He talked to Uriel a few more moments before finally ending the call. He then called his parents and another one of his men who was following Johnny Rush. He discovered Rush had spent the night at a bar, probably drowning in grief since he didn't know the whereabouts of Danielle Simone.

York placed his phone back on the table and headed for the kitchen, deciding Darcy deserved breakfast in bed.

A police siren sounded in the distance and woke Darcy. She opened her eyes to the glare of the bright sunlight shining into the bedroom window and glanced around, immediately remembering where she was and whose bed she was in.

She shifted and immediately felt the tenderness between her legs, which was a blatant reminder of all the lovemaking she'd participated in the night before. Had she really made love on a raft in the sea? And on the beach? Jeez.

And she couldn't forget how they'd come inside later to shower together and ended up doing that and a whole lot more. She recalled how they'd slept during the night with his body spooning hers.

She lay on her side to glance out the window, and all she could see was the beautiful blue-green water. Waking up to such a sight was simply awesome.

She heard movement downstairs and immediately felt the quickened beats of her heart. What had brought her and York to this? Why even now she had to admit that he had to be the most generous of lovers . . . and the most skilled. The man didn't miss beat when it came to pleasuring a woman. He had mastered the skills. It was certainly an ingrained talent that some men never gained. After making love with him she doubted she could ever turn to the likes of Bruce again for anything.

And now that she'd apologized for her behavior of two years ago, they were getting along. At least they were when neither of them mentioned Damien Felder. She knew York suspected the man of wrongdoing, but she was of the mind that a man was innocent until proven guilty. All it took was to remember what had happened to her father years ago when Darcy had been in her early teens.

Her father was a high school teacher, and one of his female students had accused him of inappropriate behavior toward her. Matlock Owens was about to lose his job as well as the respect of the community before the young girl tearfully admitted she had lied just to get attention from her parents. The girl and her family, totally embarrassed by what they'd done, had eventually moved away, but it had taken years before the Owens family had gotten over what had been done to them. Darcy, who'd always been a "daddy's girl," had seen firsthand what the false accusations had done to her father and didn't want the same thing to happen to Damien.

She knew York assumed she was defensive of Damien because she was interested in him, but that was not the case. And in a way she shouldn't really care what York thought. But for some reason she did.

"You're awake."

She turned to the sound of York's voice. He was standing in the doorway with a breakfast tray in his hand. She couldn't help but smile. No man had ever treated her to breakfast in bed before. She pulled up into a sitting position, realizing she was completely naked under the covers. Where were her clothes? She recalled racing into the house naked last night, then remembered they'd left their clothes in a heap near the blanket. They'd probably gotten washed away by now.

As if reading her thoughts, York came into the room and placed the tray on the nightstand. "I got our clothes. I just shook the sand from your dress because I didn't know if it was washable. But everything else I tossed into the washing machine."

She nodded. The thought of him handling

her underthings sent flutters all through her. "Thanks."

He then glanced down at the tray. "I wasn't sure what you liked, so I brought you a little bit of everything."

He was right. It was loaded with pancakes, sausage, bacon, scrambled eggs, a bowl of fresh fruit and toast. She felt she gained five pounds just looking at all the food he'd prepared. "Thanks, and I hope you know there's no way I can eat this all by myself. You are planning to join me, right?"

He chuckled. "Right. But I need to go back for the coffee."

It was only after York had left the room that Darcy was able to breathe normally. He needed a shave but that *I-could-use-a-shave* look made him appear even sexier and more rugged. She shook her head. Ellie would never believe that she and York had called a truce long enough to toss between the sheets.

"I'm back."

Darcy glanced over at him as he entered the room. He was wearing a pair of jeans that rode low on his hips, and he was bare chested. She recalled licking every inch of that broad chest last night. She also remembered licking other parts of him as well. The scorching sensuality of her actions, as well

168

as her risqué behavior, almost entrapped her into a deep-rooted desire that could overtake her if she wasn't careful.

She watched as he placed two cups of coffee beside the breakfast tray. He then proceeded to remove his jeans before crawling back into bed with her. She quickly scooted over and made room for him. But he didn't let her go too far before pulling her close for a kiss.

Dang. No man should be able to kiss that good in the mornings. Such a thing should be outlawed. It was a kiss so arousing that her body tingled.

She was the one who finally pulled back from the kiss knowing if she didn't she would be spread eagle beneath him in no time. And as much as she didn't want to admit it, being with York could be habit-forming, and she'd never wanted to find herself addicted to any man. She was deeply attracted to him; that in itself could make her vulnerable, and she didn't want that.

"I think you need to feed me," she said lifting a finger to his jaw and rubbing the stubble there as she gazed at his mouth. He had such a beautiful pair of lips, and he definitely knew how to use them to his advantage. She would always have to be a few steps ahead of him, otherwise she would risk getting in too deep. This was a man who — if she wasn't careful and on her toes — would make her want the one thing she swore she would never want with a man again. An exclusive relationship.

He reached for the coffee and handed her a cup. "Be careful, it's hot," he said.

And so are you, she wanted to counter and decided to keep that thought to herself.

He then placed the tray of food between them and began eating off of it. Several times he actually fed pieces of bacon to her. And when he leaned in to nibble a piece of bacon off her lip she thought she would come in a full-blown orgasm then and there.

There was something she needed to ask him about, something that still bothered her although it shouldn't. "York?"

"Yes?"

"That morning after we made love in my hotel room. You left before I woke up. Why?"

He held her gaze. "Had I not left then, Darcy, I might not have left. You had a tendency to make me forget I was on the island for a reason. I had a job to do. My team needed me in place, although I wanted more than anything to stay right in your bed."

She inwardly smiled and didn't want to think how his words had her floating on a cloud of contentment. He *had* wanted to stay with her.

"Any more questions, Darcy?"

She shook her head. "No, not right now."

"Good. What do you want to do today?" he then asked her.

She took a sip of her coffee, surprised by his question. She had assumed he would be taking her back to the hotel after breakfast. She'd figured taking up his time was not an option.

"What do you suggest?" she asked him.

That I-can-think-of-a-number-of-things smile tempted her to lean over and kiss it off his lips, but she decided to refrain from doing so. "We can go back rafting today," he suggested, reminding her of what they'd done last night. "Or we can stay in, naked, and watch movies," he added.

She chuckled as she took another sip of her coffee. "Sounds interesting."

"Trust me, I can make it as interesting as you want."

She could believe that. "Don't you have work to do today? Need I remind you that you're working on a case?"

He grinned. "Need I remind you that it's the weekend? No filming today and the cast and crew have scattered. I have several men assisting me, and they are keeping dibs on those I need to keep up with."

She couldn't help but wonder if Damien was one of those. She couldn't imagine having her privacy invaded in such a way and pushed the thought to the back of her mind. Otherwise, she would speak her mind and she and York would end up arguing again. "Watching movies sounds good, but I'm not doing so in the nude. The first thing I plan on doing is washing my dress."

"You're a spoilsport, Darcy Owens," he said chuckling, a pretended pout on his lips.

They continued to eat breakfast, and he mentioned the call he'd gotten from Uriel with the news about Eli Steele. She knew Eli and his brothers through her association with Ellie and Uriel. She glanced over at York after taking another sip of her coffee. "Did you mention to Uriel that we were together?"

He met her gaze and shook his head. "No. I didn't feel it was my place, especially since he didn't mention it, which to me meant you hadn't said anything to Ellie."

She paused in chewing of a piece of sausage. "I haven't talked to Ellie since arriving. I'm due to give her a call, but I prefer not saying anything about us being together. At least not yet. El gets carried away with certain things," she said. *Especially when it's about me and a man.*

"No problem. We will handle our involvement whatever way you prefer."

Our involvement. Were they actually involved? Did their actions on two separate occasions account for an involvement? She couldn't help wondering if an involvement and a fling were basically the same thing. She considered a fling as short term and an involvement as something a little longer.

She continued to eat wondering just how he really saw their affair.

York sipped on his coffee in thoughtful silence. He couldn't get the vision out of his mind of him making love to Darcy last night — first on a raft and then later on the blanket he'd spread on the sand. Both times had been simply incredible. And he couldn't forget that night in her hotel room.

While he'd been downstairs preparing breakfast, he had found himself watching the clock, anticipating the moment she would awake. He had never felt possessive when it came to a woman, but he did so with her. He could even recall the exact moment he felt he had made her his.

He wondered how he was going to break the news to her. He'd told her at the time, while they'd been making love, but he doubted she remembered.

He had a gut feeling that Darcy was a woman that didn't want to belong to anyone. But he wanted to prove her wrong. York shook his head thinking something was wrong with him. Here he was on the island and working an important case, and the only thing he wanted to think about was making love to Darcy again. He'd thought that calling for a truce had been a good idea. He hadn't known doing so would entice him to build a relationship with a woman who had built a wall around herself. What he'd told her earlier was true. They were involved, and it was an involvement that he intended to explore to the fullest.

"This is delicious, York."

"Thanks. I enjoy being in the kitchen when I have the time. Usually I don't."

"You travel a lot?"

He glanced over at her and nodded. "Not as much as I used to when I was getting the business off the ground. Now I have people who travel for me. This case was different, though, and I wanted to be in the thick of things. One of the men who invested a lot of money into the movie production is a close friend of my father's. He's been losing a lot of money lately."

When he told her just how much, her eyes

widened as if she'd found it hard to believe. "That's a lot of money for anyone to lose on a business deal," she said.

"Yes, it is, and it bothers me to think that it's an inside job."

Darcy didn't say anything, and York knew she was thinking of Felder and whether his accusations about the man could be true. She wouldn't bring him up and neither would he. The man was a touchy subject between them, and it was best his name remained out of their conversation.

And speaking of conversation, he decided to switch things. "Have you ever ridden a Jet Ski?"

She shook her head. "No."

He smiled. "Then that's what we'll do today. I'll teach you how it's done."

"You own one?"

"Yes."

She nodded. "Sounds like fun." She then leaned over and softly kissed his lips. "Thanks for last night, York. It was wonderful."

Yes, what they'd shared had been wonderful, and he intended to spend more of such wonderful times with her.

Darcy couldn't help but smile as she watched York give her a demonstration on the proper way to use the Jet Ski. It was a beautiful piece of equipment, but then the person showing her how to use it was a beautiful man.

After breakfast they had dressed and he had taken her back to the hotel where she had packed an overnight bag and returned here. They had gone swimming for a while and now he was showing her how to use a Jet Ski, and she was having a great time watching him.

They were still wearing their swimsuits. She was wearing a fuchsia bikini, which he seemed quite taken with when she'd put it on. In fact, he'd seemed quite taken with taking it off her as well. He had stripped her naked, tossed the bikini on shore while they went skinny-dipping.

She smiled remembering that time as she studied him. His swimming trunks showed just what a fine physique he had — tight muscles, firm stomach, and thick muscular thighs. His skin was glistening from the water, and her tongue tingled, tempted to lick him dry.

"Any questions?"

She smiled upon realizing that he had asked her a question. "About what?"

He laughed and shook his head. "About anything I just went over with you."

The only thing she could remember — and rather vividly — was listing parts of his body she found fascinating. But not to give anything away, she said, "No, I don't have any questions."

"So you're ready to try it?"

She wouldn't say that. "Only if we can do it together."

That statement made him grin, and she immediately understood why. They had been practically doing it together most of the morning. Ever since she had let the cat out of the bag that she'd gone without sex for almost two years, he had definitely made himself available without any trouble, and she had readily taken him up on his offers.

After breakfast they'd made love, and when they had gotten to her hotel room after she'd thrown items into her overnight bag, they'd made love again. There was just something about him that pushed thoughts of sex to the forefront of her mind. Their lovemaking sessions were always wild and out of control, unrestrained and uncontrollable. He seemed to enjoy it that way, and so did she.

"What I meant," she decided to clarify, "is to ask if we can ride the Jet Ski together."

"We sure can. It can hold up to three people," he said, smiling over at her.

Darcy nodded. She was about to tell him how nice the brightly colored Jet Ski was when her cell phone rang.

She recognized the number and felt a deep thump in her chest. She glanced over at York and knew she didn't have to tell him who was calling. She probably had a guilty look on her face, although there was no reason for her to be guilty about anything. She had come to the island to enjoy herself and have fun. York didn't mean any more to her than Damien did.

She knew it was a lie as soon as the thought left her brain. She considered ignoring the call and then decided to go ahead and answer it, knowing full well that York would be listening to her every word. "Yes, Damien?"

"I'll be back on the island Monday night, and I was wondering when I can see you again."

CHAPTER 9

A frown settled around York's lips. Part of his brain tried convincing him that he didn't care, that whatever Darcy did and with whom was her business and that it didn't concern him. But that was a bald-faced lie. It did concern him, not just personally but physically.

He continued to wipe down his Jet Ski while trying to ignore her conversation with Felder. The man was with Danielle Simone, so why was he calling Darcy? He fought to keep his teeth from clenching and had to suck in a deep breath when he was struck by an intense urge to take the phone from her and ask him. The very thought was insane, but the one thing he wasn't feeling at the moment was sane.

Keep your cool, Ellis. Just because you and Darcy have been mating like rabbits every chance you get is no reason to get all possessive and territorial. But then again, maybe you have every right since you did claim her and decided she was yours.

He crouched down to wipe off a lower part of the Jet Ski while thinking he could bet all the tea in China that Darcy wouldn't agree with that assessment. She would probably box his ears if she even knew he had such thoughts and was making such assumptions.

He pretended not to notice when she ended the call. He tried ignoring the moment of awkward silence that followed and figured he should say something but decided considering how he felt it was best to keep his mouth shut. He was encountering emotions he'd never felt before, and he wasn't quite sure how to handle them. No woman had ever made him feel this way, and quite honestly, he didn't like it.

"That was Damien."

He glanced over at her without stopping what he was doing. "I gathered."

She didn't say anything for a moment and neither did he. A part of him wished he could concentrate on something else. For the last hour or so, he had been admiring how she looked in the bikini, appreciating her curvy figure and long legs. Now all he could see was the color red flash across his eyes.

He knew his attitude wasn't helping matters, but at the moment, he truly didn't give a damn. Standing less than five feet away was the woman he had made love with most of the night — the woman who had somehow gotten underneath his skin. He broke eye contact with her and continued his work.

"You have no right to be this way, you know."

Her words did something to him, snapped off the last of his patience. He rose to his feet and faced her. Instead of saying anything, he stepped around her and went inside through the back door. She was watching him curiously, and he knew eventually she would follow.

Once inside his kitchen, he turned the moment she swept in behind him. Before she could open her mouth, he was on her, kissing her. Every part of him was throbbing in both anger and arousal. She evidently didn't know anything about rights when it came to him. And he intended to teach her a few things.

God, he wanted her again. He wanted to wipe Damien Felder's name from her memory. He wanted to feel the way their bodies connected when they made love, feel her fingers digging deep in his shoulder blades while he rode her hard, hear her scream his name when she came. Hell, they didn't just have sex together; they had something a lot more remarkable and astonishing.

Instead of pushing him away, she gripped his shoulders and pressed her mouth even closer to him, and he took it with fierce intensity, using his tongue to seduce her to a moan.

And it seemed that she needed the kiss as much as he did when she proceeded to feast hungrily on his mouth. He lifted her up slightly, and she instinctively wrapped her legs around him. Without breaking the kiss, he began walking toward the living room. It was hot outside, but nothing could compare to the temperature he was feeling inside.

York was determined by the time things were over she would know what rights he did have.

This was madness. When he kissed her, Darcy couldn't form a coherent thought. All she knew was that if she continued to get wrapped up in York she could get hurt, because he was awakening emotions she preferred not feeling.

Darcy felt the back of her legs touch the sofa, but instead of lowering her to the sofa,

York scooped her into his arms, headed over to the desk and placed her on it. He kissed her again greedily, and she returned the kiss with the same intensity, urgency and hunger.

Moments later when York broke off the kiss to look at her, all she could do was stare into his eyes, just moments before moving her gaze to his wet lips. Then her gaze moved lower, past his bare chest to the swimming trunks. They were no longer wet, probably from all the heat being generated in that area. He was hard and enlarged, and she couldn't stop herself from reaching out and sliding her fingers inside his swimming trunks.

His erection felt hot to the touch, and she cupped him in her hand and could feel the huge veins along the head of him throbbing. She couldn't stop running her fingers along the side of his thickness, thinking he was getting even larger with each stroke.

He reached down and covered her hand with his and asked huskily, "Do you want this?"

His question was definitely a no-brainer. Yes, she wanted it. Since he asked, he evidently wanted to hear her say it and she had no problem doing so. She said, "Yes, I want it." And then because she wanted to hear his admission as well, she asked, "Do you want me?"

He released her hand and slid his own inside her bikini bottom, and then his fingers began exploring her like they had every right to do so. Instinctively, the moment he touched her feminine mound she spread her legs to give him better access. And when he touched her clit, she moaned deep in her throat.

"Oh, yeah, I want you," he whispered close to her lips and leaned over while his fingers continued to stroke her inside. Her heart pounded fiercely in her chest as sensations began overtaking her.

Every nerve inside her body began tingling. And then he leaned forward and used his teeth to lower her bikini top and bared her breasts. Before she could release a gasp of surprise, his mouth latched onto a nipple and began sucking.

Darcy tossed her head back when she felt unbearably hungry for him. Her body was craving him with an intensity that shocked her.

Suddenly he released her to take a step back, and she was forced to let go of him as well. She drew in a deep breath when he eased his swimming trunks down his legs after removing a condom packet from the pocket. She loved a man who believed in being prepared. She then watched as he sheathed his erection, forcing herself to swallow during the process.

He returned to her, and she assumed he would take her off the desk. Instead, he lifted her hips and proceeded to remove her bikini, tossing both somewhere behind him. "You like undressing me, don't you?" she asked in a trembling voice. They had made love several times before, but with York, she never knew what to expect. There was never a dull moment with him when it came to making love — in or out of the bedroom.

"Yes," was his husky response, and before she could say anything else, he lowered his head to her breasts again.

She moaned and lifted her hand to stroke the side of his face, close to his mouth, and she could feel how hard he was sucking her breasts. It caused a myriad of sensations to invade the area between her legs. He had a way of making her feel desired and wanted.

And then he released her nipple, and before she could move, he lifted her hips just seconds before lowering his head between her legs. The second his tongue touched her clit, sensations rammed through her, and she let out a deep moan. He began tonguing her as if she would be his last meal, as if he was intent on exploring every single inch of her satiny flesh.

"York!"

Instead of answering her, he pulled her body closer to his mouth, and his tongue delved even deeper. She'd never felt this aroused in her entire life. He was doing something with his tongue, drawing little circles inside of her, especially on her G-spot.

She felt an orgasm coming on and tried pushing him away, but just as he'd done the last time he had performed oral sex on her, he remained unmovable, unstoppable. Sensations exploded inside of her, and her entire body shook in extreme pleasure. His mouth closed deeper on her and his tongue continued to lave her clit, and her orgasm seemed endless. A rush of heat infused her, and she couldn't help screaming out his name when more and more explosions shattered her body.

"Damn, you taste good," he said moments later when he raised his head and smiled at her. Before she could give him a response, he had grabbed her by the hips and eased her toward his waiting erection. It felt hot when it brushed against her thigh and when he was easing it inside of her. Immediately, her inner muscles clamped down on his pulsating erection. He went deep and deeper, until she could feel his testicles resting against her flesh. He filled her so completely, so totally, she didn't think he had room to move inside.

He proved her wrong when he began stroking her, easing out and going back in, making sensations rush through her veins and pour into her bloodstream. She was convinced she felt him all the way to her womb, and she knew for certain that her body could feel every hard inch of him.

His strokes seemed urgent, and her inner muscles began milking him, needing to keep him inside her for as long as she could. The more he pounded into her, the deeper he seemed to go and the more she wanted him. He lifted her hips, held them tight and steady to receive each and every one of his hard thrusts.

"Tell me, Darcy," she heard him say. "Tell me this gives me the right. Tell me."

She bit down on her mouth, not wanting to say the words he wanted to hear. She had made love to other men and would have thrown such a request back in their face. But she knew he was right. No other man had made love to her like York did or could. No other man could make her womanhood contract with such intense pleasure.

But should that alone give him the right to anything when it came to her? Oh, hell, she thought, when he increased his pace and began pounding into her with an intensity that almost left her speechless. To get this type of pleasure she would give him whatever rights he thought he wanted.

"York!"

She screamed his name and felt her entire body tremble when an orgasm tore into her. And she knew at that moment what else she wanted, what else she wanted to feel. If he was demanding rights from her then she wanted what she considered as the ultimate in pleasure.

When he pushed hard inside of her and then retreated to thrust back into her, she shifted her body to ease away slightly. Before he realized what she was doing, she reached out and tugged the condom off his erection and tossed it to the floor. She looked at him and said, "With rights come sacrifices. I want you to let go inside of me. I want to feel your semen."

Darcy didn't have to ask twice. Before she could draw in her next breath, York was back inside of her, skin to skin, and he felt the difference all the way to his toes. Hell, he wanted her to feel his semen as well.

There was something about her that had his erection throbbing mercilessly inside of her. That had pressure building up inside him just for the purpose of exploding inside of her. He began stroking her again, almost nonstop.

"Oh, baby, I'm coming." He leaned forward to claim her mouth the moment his body exploded, blasting hot semen inside of her and rocking his entire body from head to toe. This was lovemaking as it should be, lovemaking as it was for him and Darcy. They had made a deal, and both had delivered. At least he had given her what she wanted, and he intended to get what he wanted — rights with her.

He broke off the kiss and threw his head back when he kept coming. Rocking his hips against her to go deeper, he knew he was branding her in a way that he had never branded a woman before. He knew the first time they'd made love there had been a chance some of his semen might have escaped inside of her, but this time he knew for certain.

He had intentionally flooded her with his seed, not for a baby but because she had asked for it. And he knew at that moment he would just about give Darcy Owens anything she wanted. And when she screamed out her orgasm it triggered another one within him, and he shot off inside of her again.

At that moment he knew that no matter how she felt about it, he would not give Damien Felder the chance to ever touch her this way or any other way.

CHAPTER 10

Darcy came awake and glanced out the window. It was still light outside, which meant it was still the same day. She inhaled the scent of sex. She glanced around the room and saw she was in York's bed, and all she had to do was close her eyes to remember when he had brought her in here.

It had been right after he'd made love to her on the desk. He had gathered her naked body into his arms and taken her into his bedroom where he had placed her in the bed. He had joined her there, stroked her body all over with the pads of his fingers to bring her to another aroused state before straddling her to make love to her again.

His arms tightened around her, and she knew he was awake as well and then he was tugging her closer to him, shifting her on her back and taking possession of her mouth. Only York could kiss her this way and make her want to demand things from a man she'd never demanded before — like his semen.

He released her mouth and stared down at her. "While you were asleep, I've been thinking," he said. His gaze was intense.

She lifted a brow. "About what?"

"Why Damien is so determined to keep you within his reach."

She released a frustrated breath. A part of her wanted to clobber him for bringing up the other man at a time like this, and a part of her wanted to reach up and wrap her arms around his neck to kiss the other man's name from his lips.

"Why are you bringing him up? I gave you rights while we're together on the island. I won't be seeing him or talking to him. Isn't that what you wanted?"

He nodded slowly. "Yes, but there are still unanswered questions in my mind."

"What kind of unanswered questions, York?"

He released a deep sigh and rubbed his hand down his face before sitting up. "My men and I have been keeping close tabs on Felder, and I haven't told you everything."

She lifted a confused brow. "Everything like what?"

"Like the fact that as soon as he parts company with you, he seeks out Danielle

Simone or vice versa. Something is going on with those two."

She shrugged. "If you think you were sparing my feelings by not telling me, you were wrong. The thought that he was hitting on her or any other woman for that matter doesn't bother me. He and I never slept together. We didn't as much as share a kiss. In my book, I was doing something that could be considered worse. I was talking to him and making love to you, a man who was having him investigated."

"That might be true, but I still think he sought you out for another reason."

She rolled her eyes. "And what reason is that?"

"To use you as a decoy to get something off this island. Has he given you anything to keep for him?"

"No. I wouldn't take anything from him."

He nodded slowly. "And you're sure he hasn't slipped anything into your purse without your knowledge?"

"No, I keep my purse on me at all times, so he wouldn't have gotten the chance." A frown then marred her forehead when she remembered something. "However, Damien did give me one of those tote bags that promoted the movie before we left the set that day. But it was empty."

"You sure of that?"

"Yes." And then she shook her head and pulled herself up in bed. "At least it felt empty. I didn't look inside of it."

"Where is it now?"

"Back at the hotel."

He was easing out of bed. "Do you mind if I take a look at it?"

Darcy shook her head, not wanting to believe he was starting back up on his mistrust of Damien all over again. "I'm going to ask you one more time, York. Why is it you want to nail everything on Damien? Why are you so convinced he's guilty of anything?"

He didn't answer immediately. Instead, he walked over to the window and glanced out. Moments later, he turned around and said, "A woman who meant a lot to me was killed when she accidentally stumbled into a robbery. Recently I found out one of the men Felder is associated with is someone the authorities believed set things up that night. There was not enough proof to arrest him. If that's true, I might be able to solve two cases, and one is deeply personal."

Darcy didn't say anything for a moment as she absorbed everything he said. She recalled everything Ellie had told her about the woman he was to marry and how she'd gotten killed.

"So what about you?" he asked. "Why are you so hell-bent on believing Felder is innocent?"

She drew in a deep breath. "I believe a person is innocent until proven guilty."

She then told him what had happened with her father while she was growing up. "So you see, York, my father was accused of something he didn't do, and I saw what it did to him. I don't want any part of doing something similar to another human being."

He nodded slowly. "I understand, Darcy, and would love to tell you I might be wrong about Felder but I don't think that I am. He has too many ties to unsavory individuals."

He glanced at his watch. "I want to check out that bag he gave you."

Darcy eased out of bed, met his unwavering gaze and sighed. "Fine. Give me a few minutes to shower and get dressed and then we can leave. But don't be surprised if you discover you're just wasting your time."

It didn't take any time getting back to the hotel. York was well aware that Darcy thought he was wasting his time and that might very well be the case, but he refused to leave any stone unturned. Someone was sneaking footage off the set some way, and he intended to find out if his hunch was right.

York slid his hands into the pockets of his jeans after they entered Darcy's hotel room, and he closed the door behind them. His gaze drifted her over as she moved in the sunlight coming in through the windows. She was wearing a short denim skirt and a cute zebra-print midriff blouse that showed a lot of skin. He could vividly recall how his hands had moved over every inch of her body, touching her, caressing her, igniting heat wherever he touched and eliciting her whimpers and moans.

He had liked the sound of her calling his name. He had liked it even more when she'd reciprocated and touched him all over, making his body quiver beneath the contact of her hands to his flesh.

Since he'd told her what he thought Felder was up to, she had a no-nonsense air about her. At least he now understood why she'd always come to the man's defense. After what had happened to her dad he could understand her trying to defend anyone she felt was being falsely accused. But he hadn't told her everything about Felder. The man had all the reasons for wanting to make a little bit of extra money on the side, even if it was at York's client's expense.

It took him a moment to realize Darcy had said something. "Sorry, could you repeat that?" he asked.

A frown appeared between her neatly arched eyebrows. "I said the tote bag is in the bedroom. I had already packed it up with my stuff since I wouldn't be using it. I'll go and get it."

He thought about following her in that bedroom and decided that wouldn't be a good idea. He might be tempted to toss her on that bed and make love to her, which was definitely something he enjoyed doing. Being around her was pure torture. If her touch didn't get to him then her scent definitely did.

He moved away from the door and crossed the room to the sliding glass doors to look out. If his theory was right then Darcy wasn't in any real danger; however, the thought that anyone, especially Felder, was using her made his teeth clench again.

There was something about her that brought out not only his protective instincts but his possessive instincts as well. A part of him just didn't know what to make of it when he'd never acted this way around other women. He needed to be in better control of his emotions since for the first time ever they seemed to be getting the best of him.

"Here's the bag, and just like I assumed, York, it's empty."

He slowly turned from the window. He tried to focus on the canvas tote bag she was holding in her hand but instead he concentrated on her hands, and he recalled just where those hands had touched him, all the things those hands had done to him.

His gaze roamed over her, and he thought today the same thing he thought every time he saw Darcy. She was a beautiful woman — beautiful and striking. The sunlight highlighted her creamy brown skin and the luster of her dark hair.

He took the tote bag to check for himself. Carrying the bag over to a table, he heard her sigh of frustration when she followed him.

"I hope you don't plan to rip my bag apart trying to find something that's probably not there, York," she said with a degree of agitation in her tone.

He merely glanced over at her and smiled. "If I have to, I'll make sure you get another one." Although he knew he was petty and childish, he didn't like the thought of her stressing out over a bag Felder had given her.

He knew she had gotten really upset with him when she left his side and sat down on the sofa. He glanced over at her and met her gaze and saw the fire in her eyes. She'd gotten uptight again, and when they got back to his place, he would look forward to loosening her up a bit.

From his pocket he pulled out what to a layman looked like an ink pen. The tip of the pen had a scanning light, and he slowly skimmed it across the bag. He smiled when the tip began blinking. He turned to Darcy and said, "According to this scanner, Darcy, this bag isn't empty."

She was off the sofa in a flash. "That's not possible," she said adamantly as she came to stand beside him, giving him more than a whiff of her luscious scent.

"We'll see," he said as he glanced back down at the tote bag. It looked empty and it felt empty, as well. Evidently there was a secret compartment somewhere in the bag. He flipped it inside out and didn't see anything suspicious. He then began feeling around and still didn't detect anything. Whatever was being hidden was a small object.

Using the scanning pen again, he skimmed

it over the bag, and when the light turned red over a certain area York smiled again. Bingo. He glanced back over at her. "Like I said earlier, I'll get you another bag."

With that said, he reached into his back pocket to retrieve a pocketknife and sliced through the seam. "What do we have here?" he asked when two memory cards slid out.

Darcy inched closer, and he noted the surprised expression on her face. Her eyes had widened, and her mouth had fallen open. "I don't believe it," she said in both disbelief and anger.

"Seeing is believing, baby. Now if we had a video camera we could see just what's on here, although I have an idea."

"I have a video camera." With that said, she rushed off toward the bedroom.

He held up the memory cards in his hand to study them. Filming had just begun, so he couldn't imagine anyone collecting too much footage yet.

He looked up when Darcy reentered the room carrying her video camera. "Nice camera," he said, when she handed it over to him.

"Thanks. It was a birthday present from my oldest brother."

He slipped in the memory card, and they watched the screen flare to life. "Whoa!"

Flashed before them was footage of the scenes being shot for Spirit Head Productions. "I don't believe this!" Darcy gasped in anger. "Felder is ripping off the company."

York clicked off the camera. "Looks that way," he said, barely able to contain his anger. "Do you know what would have happened to you if these were found in your possession by anyone?"

He could tell by her expression that she knew the seriousness of the predicament Felder had placed her in. And he could also tell that the more she thought about it the angrier she was becoming.

"I can't wait to see him, and when I do I'll —"

"Say nothing," he said with a dark scowl. "I tried to warn you about him, but you wouldn't take heed to my warning."

She lifted her chin. "I know that, York, and I regret not doing so, but not saying anything to him is not an option."

"It has to be," he said. "Calm down and think for a minute. Felder believes that you're clueless that he's using you as a decoy to get these back into the States. Now I'm curious as to who is supposed to get these. I'm sure it's probably not anyone you know, so when was he going to get the bag from you? Who is it going to? And who —"

"And you think I give a royal flip about any of that?" she asked fuming. "If I would have gotten arrested returning from vacation carrying those memory cards I might as well have kissed my job goodbye. I can imagine the article that would have appeared in the papers, the embarrassment it would have caused my family."

"But you would have been innocent."

"Yes, just like my dad had been innocent — but the humiliation almost killed him," she said furiously.

York knew she was taking in the blunt reality of what could have happened and he understood. Now it was imperative that he make her understand something as well. "But you've been spared all of that, Darcy. Think of the next person he might use. Think about how Felder and his accomplices are getting away with it."

He knew his words had gotten to her when she lowered her head to study the floor. Her breathing indicated she was still upset and angry. But at least he had gotten her to start thinking. "Just think about it, Darcy. I'll have a chance to nail this guy and his associates for good."

She lifted her head and met his gaze head on. "Correction, York. *We'll* have a chance to nail them. I'm the one he's set up to take the fall if anything went wrong."

She didn't say anything for a moment and then added, "But he's counting on nothing going wrong. Now I'm just as curious as you as to who is supposed to take this bag off me. I wouldn't just meekly turn it over to anyone."

York's expression was mixed with wariness and caution. "What do you mean 'we'?"

"Just what I said. In order for you to find out who this bag was meant for and how they plan to get it, I'll need to be a player in all this."

He crossed his arms over his chest and stared down at her. "No, you don't. Now that you know the truth about Felder, I want you to bow out of the picture."

Darcy shook her head. "No, I won't do that. I'm keeping that bag."

"And risk going to jail?"

"Then I guess it will be up to you to make sure I don't," she replied as she brought her face close to his.

That wasn't the only thing close. Her breasts were now pushed up to his chest. Desire as thick as it could get suddenly rushed through his veins. All sorts of scenarios entered his mind of what could go wrong if he went along with what she was proposing. But at that moment, he couldn't think. Lust was taking over, and logical thoughts couldn't compete.

He leaned forward, and he growled close to her lips before he took her mouth with all the hunger he felt.

Darcy knew she wasn't thinking sensibly. But she hadn't thought sensibly since she'd planned this trip. She had wanted action and a man, and by golly she was getting them both in the form of York Ellis. And the way he was kissing her was making her realize she was one lucky woman.

No man could kiss the way he did. No other male had his taste. And she was totally convinced that no man's tongue could do all the things that his could. He'd told her at breakfast that he thought her mouth was made for kissing. Well, she thought his was, too.

He was kissing her with a sexual tempo, a seductive rhythm that had her moving her body even closer to his. They didn't just fit together, she thought. They fit together perfectly. She could feel the hard tips of her nipples press against the T-shirt he was wearing.

And that wasn't all she was feeling. She knew the moment his hands cupped her backside to make them an even more perfect fit. She liked the way his huge and hard erection was nestled at the juncture of her thighs and the way his breathing sounded while he was kissing her.

Heat rushed through her bloodstream. She wasn't surprised when he lifted up the hem of her jeans skirt and with eager fingers explored underneath.

She moaned deep in her throat when those same fingers came in contact with her thong and moved beyond them to her satiny folds. He dipped his fingers in her wetness, and she gripped his shoulders to keep from tumbling in desire.

She pulled her mouth from his and moaned out his name. "York."

"I want to take you into that bedroom, strip you naked and lick you all over."

His words had her mind, her senses and her entire body spinning. She met the heated gaze. "If you get to do it to me then I get to do it to you. Is that a deal?"

He smiled. "Hell, yeah." He then swept her off her feet and carried her into the bedroom.

Darcy's heart pounded hard in her chest. She had never made love in this position. She was straddling York's face and he was straddling hers, and the moment his tongue slid inside of her she nearly lost it. Every nerve in her body responded, and when he began feasting on her clit, she moaned deep in her throat.

And that's when she knew she needed to taste him the same way he was tasting her. Her fingers gripped his erection and brought it to her mouth. She began devouring him the same way he was devouring her. She could feel the strength of him throb in her throat, expand in her mouth, thicken around her tongue.

She loved the taste of him, and she loved what he was doing to her, how he was making her feel. Some type of movement that he did with his tongue made her moan out loud. What was he doing to her? To retaliate, she deepened her hold on him, and he rocked his hips against her mouth when she rocked hers against his.

She felt sensations burst to life inside her belly and knew what was about to happen. She sank her mouth deeper on him when her body exploded about the same time that his did. And she applied even more pressure on him to absorb the very essence of him like he was doing with her.

It seemed as if this orgasm for the both of them was endless and they rode it out, satisfying their taste buds as he filled her the way she was filling him.

Moments later, he rolled away from her, and she was forced to let him go. He faced her, then straddled her again and slid into her still wet warmth.

"York."

"Darcy."

And then he began thrusting inside of her. Hard. Penetrating. Deep. With every hard stab, every delicious pounding, she groaned. He was filling her, going deeper and deeper, and her greedy inner muscles were gripping him, clenching him, demanding he give her now what he'd shot into her mouth moments ago.

He lifted his head to stare down at her while the lower part of his body continued to ride her. "Like it?"

"Love it."

He smiled, and that smile coming from York sent pleasure reeling all through her. "You're mine, Darcy."

She heard his words, and for the moment she couldn't argue with him. At that moment, she and every part of her being were his. He was giving her insurmountable pleasure and she felt it from the top of her head to the soles of her feet, and when another explosion took its toll on her, she knew one thing was for certain. She knew she would never play around with a sex toy again. Not when she could have the real thing from York Ellis.

CHAPTER 11

"York, you are definitely a bad boy."

York smiled as he shifted to his side to gaze down at her. She sounded out of breath, like she could get barely get the words out, like she had gotten worn out. He was filled with male pride that he was the reason.

"A bad boy?" he asked, holding her gaze.

"Oh, yes, definitely bad. I've never done anything like that before. In fact, I've never done half the stuff I've done with you. Who makes love on the beach or in a raft for heaven's sake?"

He chuckled. "A man hard up for the woman he's with."

She smiled as if pleased with his answer. "And were you hard up for me?"

"Baby, I'm hard up for you now." He knew there was no way she could not believe what he'd said with the strength of his erection resting against her thigh, throbbing like it hadn't come a few times already.

"Now to get back to the subject we were discussing earlier," she said softly.

He shook his head. "I don't recall us discussing anything."

She gently punched him in his arm. "Liar. If I have to, I will refresh your memory. And speaking of memory, it was about those memory cards."

York didn't say anything for a moment. He had hoped she had somehow forgotten about that but should have known better. He reached down and swept a lock of hair off her forehead and said softly, "Let me handle it, Darcy."

She held his gaze. "I appreciate you wanting to, but I'm the one Felder figured to use. I owe him."

York pulled in a deep breath. He'd heard about a woman scorned, but he had a feeling a woman a man had set out to use would be just as resentful and spiteful. She would also be revengeful, and that's what he didn't have time for. He didn't need her or anyone else getting in the way of him bringing down Felder and whoever he was working for and with. "Darcy, I want you to let me handle it. Let it go."

"I can't."

He heard the seriousness in her voice and

realized at that moment she truly couldn't. Then he again remembered what she'd told him about her father. She was a woman wronged, and she intended — come hell or high water — to get even. At that moment, he truly felt sorry for Felder.

But still, York decided to try to appeal on her logical side, to get her to back away from the unknown. He had some names of those Felder might be in cahoots with and expected there might be others. The bootlegged films would bring in a lot of money and would possibly bankrupt the production company. It wasn't fair that many people would lose their jobs due to shameless greed.

"You have got to let me do this, York."

Her words regained his attention, and he glanced down at her, saw the determination in her eyes. "This is not a game, Darcy. It's serious business. You don't know the type of men we're dealing with. You could get hurt." He came short of saying she could lose her life. He thought about Rhonda, how her life had ended and she had been trained to take down the bad guys. But a bullet had stopped her, anyway.

"Yes, but think about it for a moment. They'd singled me out as their fall guy. Supposedly, without my knowledge, they have

211

given me something to pass on to someone. But who? How is the contact supposed to be made? Why was I singled out? All we know is someone is supposed to get those memory cards. But when? I think I should go along pretending that business is usual and see how this plays out. I'm just as capable as any female employee you might bring in. Have you forgotten I can defend myself?"

No, he hadn't forgotten. He knew she was trained in martial arts. And from what he'd heard she was pretty good. But still, karate couldn't stand a chance against a gun aimed at you with a bullet destined to kill you.

He rubbed his hand down his face and then said, "Let me think about this."

She nodded, but again he saw the determined look in her eyes. Regardless of what his decision might be, she'd already made hers. "Did Felder say when he'll be back?" he asked her.

"Yes. He said he was returning Monday and wanted to see me again."

He thought for a second and then said, "That tote bag isn't something you would automatically bring with you, and he knows you'll probably get suspicious if you were asked about it. He plans to get it some other way. And I don't think it will be on this island. I believe he plans for someone to get it from you when you get back to Miami. I think he just wants to keep up with you while you're here on the island. Those videos are worth a lot of money, and he'll want to keep tabs on them."

"Let him."

"Did you ever mention to him how long you'll be on the island?" he asked.

"Yes, that night he took me to dinner and dancing. He also knows that I have a few hours layover in Miami before flying on to Minnesota."

York nodded slowly. "Come on, let's get up, get dressed and go back to my place. We can think some more there."

But it wasn't thinking that he wanted to do. He wanted nothing more than to make love to her again. And more than anything, he wanted to keep her safe from men like Felder. But he knew she wouldn't appreciate his protection. She would see it as a weakness on her part.

He eased his naked body out of bed and glanced around the room for his jeans. "Can I ask you something, York?" He heard her say.

He turned his attention to her. "Yes."

"How do you manage to stay hard for so

213

long? Even when you don't have sex on your mind?"

Of all the things he had expected her to ask, that wasn't it and he couldn't help his quick laugh. But then he really shouldn't be surprised. Darcy did have the tendency to speak her mind. "And what makes you think I don't have sex on my mind?" he countered.

She shrugged beautiful naked shoulders. "I just figured you didn't."

He smiled. "You're lying in bed naked and you think I don't have sex on my mind? Less than an hour after I got to perform one of my fantasy positions?"

A smile curved her lips. "That was your fantasy position?"

"Yes, but I have several."

She pushed the bedcovers aside exposing her nakedness. "Show me another one. I'm game."

The pulse at the base of his throat was fluttering erratically as he raked his gaze over her. He thought she was simply beautiful whether she was in clothes or out of them. Lying there naked in bed, looking more gorgeous than any woman had a right to look made him get harder and thicker. He wasn't surprised she noticed that as well.

"You're getting even more aroused, York.

There's no need letting a good, hard erection go to waste, is there?"

He truly liked the way she thought. "No, there's not," he said and headed back to the bed.

They had been back at York's beach house less than ten minutes when Darcy's cell phone rang. York had gone outside to put away the Jet Ski and set up the grill. She smiled when she saw her caller was Ellie. She was glad her friend was not there to see the deep blush that suddenly appeared on her features. If Ellie knew what she'd been doing for the past few days and with whom, she wouldn't believe her.

"Hello."

"Hey, girl, just thought I'd give you a warning. Uriel mentioned at dinner that York is also on the island."

Darcy smiled. Everyone in their inner circles knew of her and York's dislike of each other and would probably be shocked, surprised as hell to discover they liked each other after all. In fact, she would go so far to say they liked each other a lot.

Their last escapade in her hotel room had turned into a sex game for them, one she had enjoyed. She hadn't known there were so many naughty ways to have fun with one's lover.

Lover.

Yes, he was definitely her lover . . . at least while she was here on the island. She knew once they returned to New York that it would be business as usual, although she doubted she could draw enough energy not to like him again. She liked him way too much now. What woman wouldn't like a man who could make her head spin, her knees go weak and her toes curl? A man who had the ability to dish out multiple orgasms?

"Darcy?"

"Yes?"

"Why aren't you saying anything? I expected you to have sent out a few colorful curse words by now, especially since you and York can't get along."

And under any normal circumstances when it came to York, she would have. But that was before she had discovered a lot more about him, including some things not connected to the bedroom. Over the past couple of days, they had talked a lot over dinner, breakfast and when they weren't busy blowing each other's minds in the bedroom. She believed he was a great brother, as great as her two, and a girl couldn't ask for more than that.

She also believed he was a natural born protector. That was evident in the way he was still trying to talk her out of any involvement with those memory cards.

And she would even go so far as to admit that once you got to know him, he was a likable person, a lot of fun to be around and wonderful company. He was well versed on a lot of things. She liked the fact that they shared the same political party, held strong in their belief there was a God and thought no matter how old he got, Prince was the bomb.

"Darcy!"

She snapped to attention. "What?"

"What's the matter with you?" Then in a low voice, Ellie asked, "Did I catch you at a bad time?"

Darcy smiled. "If you're asking if you caught me with my panties off and in bed with a man, then the answer is no. But had you called an hour or so earlier the answer would be a resounding yes!"

"You are protecting yourself, right?"

She swallowed deeply. "Yes, I am protecting myself."

She knew why Ellie was asking. Ellie was the only person who knew how much she enjoyed the feel of a man's release erupting inside of her. That had always been a deep, dark fantasy of hers — one she could never indulge in with a man. It had been okay with her and Harold when they were married, but after her divorce she could never trust any man to go that far with her.

But she trusted York. She believed he was in good health like he believed she was. He had told her he didn't make it a point to make love to a woman without a condom, regardless of whether she was on any type of birth control or not. Too many women out there were looking for some man to become their baby's daddy, and he did not want that status. However, he didn't mind letting go inside of her. In fact, she would probably be safe to say he enjoyed giving it as much as she enjoyed getting it.

"So you've met a man . . ."

Ellie's statement reclaimed her attention. She decided to be honest. "Yes, I've met a man."

"Is he someone from the islands?" Ellie asked.

"No."

"American?"

"Yes."

"I don't have to ask if he's nice looking," Ellie tacked on.

Darcy smiled. "No, you don't have to ask. And don't bother asking if he's good in bed because he is. And yes, he was well worth my two years of abstinence."

There was a pause on the other end, and then Ellie asked quietly, "Is he someone you can see yourself falling in love with, Darcy?"

At that moment, Darcy's heart literally sank from her chest right into the pit of her stomach. Ellie's question hit her like a ton of bricks and made her realize something she had tried not to think about. She had come to the island for fun and sex but not love. Love had been a word that had gotten torn from the pages of her memory the day she'd divorced Harold. Love was an emotion she hadn't thought about since the day she had refused to take any more of her ex's foolishness, and had come to the realization that she could do bad all by herself and that he wasn't worth the heartache.

But now thanks to Ellie that one word was back, and all the emotions that came with it were staring her right smack in the face. And the sad thing was that she knew the answer to her best friend's question. Yes, York was someone she could see herself falling in love with, and heaven help her, she was almost there. It wouldn't take much to push her over the edge and get her heart screwed up all over again.

She rubbed her hand down her face. How

could she have let it happen? When did it happen? Was it too late to pull back and run in the opposite direction?

"You've taken too long to answer, Dar. Should I include another place setting at the New Year's Eve dinner party?"

She closed her eyes, trying to force her body, her mind, her thoughts into denial. York was just her island lover. When they returned to New York, things would go back to how they were before. Her mind could agree with that reasoning but her heart was playing hardball.

Darcy drew in a deep breath, knowing why. She would want to continue to play all those naughty and fun games with him. She couldn't imagine being in the same room with him and not being able to plan their next sexual escapade. And she refused not to be able to kiss him, tangle her tongue with his, suck on it as if she had every right.

Rights.

He wanted rights when it came to her, and hadn't she given them to him to some degree? Did he expect those rights to extend beyond Jamaica? Would it truly bother her if he did expect it? She shook her head knowing it would probably bother her if he didn't.

"Maybe I need to call you back later. Sounds like I've given you a lot to think about," Ellie said, once again interrupting Darcy's thoughts.

"Yes, you have."

"And when you call me back you will let me know if I should add another name to my guest list, right?" Ellie said.

Darcy forced a chuckle. She was one hundred percent certain her lover's name was already on the guest list. But she wasn't ready to tell Ellie that yet. "Yes, I'll let you know then."

Moments later, she hung up the phone. Ellie was right. She had been given a lot to think about.

Chapter 12

"It's a good thing you discovered those memory cards on Ms. Owens, York," Wesley Carr was saying. "There's a chance she would have cleared security like Felder counted on her doing. But what if she hadn't?"

York leaned against the shed in his backyard and rubbed a hand down his face as his talked to Wesley on his cell phone. That scenario Wesley had just mentioned was one he really and truly didn't want to think about. It would have been hard for her to convince anyone that those memory cards had been planted on her and that she knew nothing about having them.

"I know, Wesley. And she's determined to let Felder think he's using her and has her just where he wants her. I'm just curious to know how he intends to get that tote bag from her."

York released a deep breath. Unknowns

were what had his gut twisting when several scenarios flashed across his mind. He didn't like a single one of them since all of them placed Darcy in some sort of danger. And all he had to do was think of what had happened to Rhonda to know he had no intention of letting that happen.

"Where is the tote bag now?" Wesley asked.

"We brought it back from the hotel, and it's here at my place."

"So what's your plan, son?"

York couldn't help but smile. Wesley personified the saying "Once a cop always a cop." "Don't know. But what I do know is that I don't want Darcy Owens placed in any danger."

"And we will work hard to make sure that doesn't happen. You got good men and women working for you."

York knew that to be true. But still . . .

There had to be that *but* in there somewhere, and he didn't like it. And of course Darcy was trying to make things complicated. She should have taken his advice from the jump and not become involved with Felder. But the stubborn woman refused to do so, and now she had the nerve to want to help him nail the guy. Well, he had news for her. Things would not go down that way. He couldn't take the chance.

"York, you still there?"

It was then that York remembered he had Wesley on the phone. "Yes, Wesley, I'm still here. I'll check in with Marlon to see how things are going with Johnny Rush. He seemed put out that Danielle Simone is missing."

"I guess he would be when it appears that she and Felder have a thing going on right under the man's nose. In my day, a man found the woman he wanted and settled down with her. Nowadays you young people shy away from commitment. Why is that, York?"

York knew he couldn't speak for others, only for himself. "Marriage isn't easy to deal with anymore, Wesley." He then thought about Rhonda. He had planned to ask her to marry him Christmas night. Her untimely death had shown him you couldn't take much for granted. It had also made him vow never to fall for another woman who didn't mind putting herself in a dangerous position.

So why was he falling for Darcy?

And he would admit that he was falling for her big time. It wasn't just the sex, although he would be the first to admit any time he was inside of her was off the chain.

But there was a side of her he hadn't gotten to know until recently when he'd begun spending time with her. Besides being sexy, she was witty and fun to be around.

"I'll check in with the others. As you know, Felder and Simone aren't the only ones I'm keeping a close eye on. I have a feeling there are others in this game of deceit. And I think it's time we need to move to plan B. And fast."

A few moments later, York had ended his conversation with Wesley and was about to go back inside his house when he got another call. This one was from his god-brother Zion to say he would be returning to the States for the holidays since Ellie insisted he attend her New Year's party.

They talked a little while, and Zion brought him up to date on how the jewelry business was doing. His hand-made jewelry was now on every woman's wish list, after the president had purchased a few pieces for the first lady. Moments later, he hung up the phone thinking he had left Darcy to her own devices way too long. It was time for him to go check on her. And time to come up with a game plan to get any ideas out of her mind of working with him to bring Felder down.

■ ■ ■ ■

"So what's our game plan, York?"

York glanced up from his breakfast and looked across the table at Darcy. Yesterday they had gone swimming and later he had treated her to grilled trout, a salad, roasted corn on the cob and ice cold lemonade. As before, she had sat at the kitchen counter and watched him work. She had volunteered to pitch in to help, but he'd convinced her his kitchen was a one-man show and that he preferred she just sit and watch him in action. She had a way of undressing him with her gaze. Usually thinking that any woman found him that interesting would annoy him, but not with Darcy — mainly because he was just as interested in her as she seemed to be in him.

And he'd proven just how much at bedtime. Memories of making love to her were still vibrant in his mind. She had surprised him upon waking up this morning. She had treated him to breakfast . . . only after treating him to something else. He'd never enjoyed early morning lovemaking so much.

He met her gaze. "Would it matter very much if I said we don't have one?" he responded while twirling his wineglass between his fingers. He had taken her up on her suggestion of swapping orange juice for wine, and he rather enjoyed it.

She gave him a sweet smile, one that didn't fool him for a minute. He'd figured it was only a matter of time for her to recall they still had a bone to pick. "Of course it would matter, York. I thought we agreed that I would be included."

He didn't want to argue with her, but he decided to try once again to make her understand why he couldn't — wouldn't — let her become involved. "We didn't agree to anything." He took a sip of his wine and then said, "I don't want anything to happen to you."

Evidently it was how he'd said it more than what he'd said that gave her pause. For the longest moment, she just stared across the table at him, and he was able to feel the intensity of her gaze. Exactly how had he said it? Then he realized it was with more emotion than he had intended.

Too late he also realized the show of emotions couldn't be helped. Darcelle Owens had literally gotten under his skin in a way no other woman had since Rhonda and in a way he'd vowed that no other woman ever would.

"Tell me about her, York."

He took another sip of his wine and played ignorant. "Tell you about who?"

"The woman you lost that meant so much to you."

There was no reason to ask how she'd heard about Rhonda. Darcy and Ellie were best friends, and somewhere along the way, Ellie had probably heard the story from Uriel, who had shared it with her . . . at least the parts Uriel knew. But there was so much more that none of his godbrothers knew — like the fact that not only had York lost the woman he had planned to marry but he'd also lost his unborn child. Rhonda had told him a week or so earlier that she was pregnant.

He liked her a lot, but he wasn't sure he had been in love with her — at least not to the extent he figured his godbrothers Uriel and Xavier were with their wives. And he had taken extreme caution each and every time they'd made love. When she'd decided to begin using the Pill, he had thought things were safe enough for him to stop using a condom. She had gotten pregnant when the antibiotics she had been taking for the flu had counteracted her birth control pills.

He had been more than willing to step up to the plate and do the right thing and marry her. However, he was certain he wouldn't have thought of marriage without the pregnancy.

"Why do you want to know anything about Rhonda?" he finally asked, placing his wineglass next to his plate after deciding he needed to be in full control of his senses when engaging in such a conversation with Darcy.

"I just do."

He held her gaze for several long moments — so long that he would not have been surprised if she withdrew her request. Of course she didn't. A part of him was tempted to tell her that her reasoning wasn't good enough, but he decided not to even bother. She had asked a question and expected a response, regardless of whether he wanted to give her one or not. York wondered if it would always be that way with them. Would there ever be a time when they would be on an even keel?

He leaned back in his chair. "Rhonda and I met about seven years ago when she joined NYPD. I had gotten out of rookie training, and she was just beginning it. We dated off and on for a while, then decided to date exclusively. We'd been at it almost eight months when she was killed."

"And you were about to ask her to marry you?"

"Yes."

She nodded slowly as if she understood everything and then she added, "You loved her that much."

He wasn't sure just what "that much" entailed, but for some reason he felt the need to set the record straight. Why he was doing it with her when he hadn't with anyone else, he wasn't sure. A slow, yet serious smile spread across his lips. Then he simply said, "No."

The room lapsed into a moment of dead silence, and he was certain he didn't hear anything. Not the sound of the waves beating against the shoreline, nor the sound of the clock on the wall ticking and not even the sound of her breathing. The look she gave him beneath silky long lashes would have him squirming in his seat had he not gotten immune to that look by now.

York watched the frown settle around her lips, and he thought that once again she looked annoyed — but not too annoyed not to ask, "And why were you planning to marry her, then?"

The answer was simple. "She was having my baby."

CHAPTER 13

Darcy sat up straight in her chair, pulled her bathrobe together when it gaped open, probably the same way her mouth did. His girlfriend had been pregnant when she'd gotten killed? Why hadn't Ellie told her that?

Evidently, that question was etched across her face because York said, "The reason Ellie didn't tell you is because she doesn't know. I've never told Uriel. No one knows. In the six years since Rhonda's death, you're the only person I've told."

Darcy wondered how she got so lucky and decided to ask. "Why tell me?"

"Because you asked."

Darcy wondered when she would learn to mind her own business. But then she recalled there was a reason for this line of conversation, and it had to do with him not wanting her to participate in exposing Felder. "I assumed the reason you didn't want me to be a part of exposing Damien is because you'd somehow feel responsible if something happened to me. Do you feel responsible for what happened to the mother of your child?"

He shook his head. "No. What she did for a living didn't bother me. I was a cop as well. I had no reason to feel responsible. We had parted that morning with plans to get together for dinner later that night. I had it all planned, a nice cozy dinner around the fireplace where I would ask her to marry me."

"But you didn't love her?"

He took another sip of his wine. "Evidently, there are several degrees of love. At the time I was in my twenties and thought I was in love but since then after hanging around Uriel and Xavier, I realized I didn't have the intense emotions toward Rhonda as they have toward their wives. If Rhonda hadn't gotten pregnant, there's no telling if the thought of marrying her would have entered my mind."

Darcy nodded. He was being honest with her, and she could appreciate that. She knew all about being in your twenties and thinking love ruled your heart and then finding out you didn't know the difference between lust and love. It had been a rude awakening for her and a period of time from which she thought she would never recover. Sometimes she wondered if she would truly ever fully recover.

"And had she lived?" Darcy heard herself prompting.

He held her gaze. "We would have married and I would have tried to be a good husband and father. But I have reason to believe we would not have made it past the five-year mark. When it came to me, she was too easy, too dead set on letting me have things my way. We rarely argued about anything because she would give in too quickly."

Darcy took a sip of her wine thinking it was just the opposite for them. Was that the reason he was attracted to her? Then what was the reason she was attracted to him besides the obvious — looks, body, his skill in the bedroom or any place you wanted to enjoy sex?

Deciding she needed to make sure he understood her position about Damien Felder, she said, "I won't be changing my mind about helping out, York."

"You'd only get in the way. Become a distraction."

She lifted both her chin and her brow. "A distraction to who?"

"Me."

She narrowed her gaze. "That sounds like a personal problem."

"It is," he agreed. "But since I can't do anything about it, I have to handle it the best way I can." He leaned closer toward her at the table. "I suggest you agree to do things my way, Darcy."

She leaned closer toward him as well. "And I suggest you do things my way, York."

He didn't as much as blink when he said, "It seems that we have a problem."

She smiled. "Like I said, it's your problem and not mine."

There was something in the way he was looking at her, holding her gaze within his dark, sharp depths that made her heart rate increase. If his eyes could talk, she knew just what they would be saying. It was evident that he was not pleased with the way things were going. She was not a "yes" girl, and he didn't very much like it. Well, that was too bad. She had no intentions of backing down.

"You know there is a simple solution to this, don't you?" he asked, still holding her gaze.

"Is there?"

"Yes, I can make sure you're out of the picture by holding you here against your will."

She smiled at the thought of that. "You don't look the type who would easily break the law."

"Then I suggest you look again."

She did. What she detected in his body language made her uneasy. "You wouldn't dare."

"You want to bet?"

No, she didn't want to bet. She wanted to leave. Standing slowly, she said, "I want to return to the hotel now."

He remained seated in his chair. His gaze was now speculative. Amused. "Running off so soon?"

She figured it was now or never. He had this way about him that attracted her way too much. Even now she felt her thighs trembling, her panties getting wet. The urge to mate with him was too intense for her comfort. If he thought he could divert her attention with something like sex . . . well, he was probably right. But she would stand firm and not let him.

"I'm going to get dressed. Are you taking me back or do I get a cab?"

"Neither."

He was serious. "I'm going to start screaming," she warned.

He chuckled. "Baby, you've been screaming a lot since you've been here, anyway."

That was true, but he didn't have to remind her or call her out on it. Her attention was drawn back to him when she heard his chair scraping against the floor, and she backed up when he stood. "Let's stop playing games, York."

"I'm not playing games, Darcy. By now, Damien has gotten word that you happened to meet an overzealous Johnny Rush fan who talked you out of your tote bag. That woman, Patricia Palmer, is an ex-cop and happens to work for me. She left the island with the tote bag in her possession this morning, headed home via a connection in Miami. My men are posted all over the Miami International Airport, along with Miami police, just waiting to see how things are going to go down."

Darcy stared at him, and when she saw he wasn't kidding and that he was dead serious, anger took over her body. "And just how did she get my tote bag?"

He crossed his arms over his chest, looking smug. "I gave it to her last night. She dropped by while you were asleep."

And because he knew how her mind worked, York added, "And no, I did not make love to you to the point of exhaustion for that reason, Darcy. Making love with

236

that much intensity and vigor is normal for us."

She slowly rounded the table and crossed the room to him. "You had no right to give what was mine to someone else," she said seething between clenched teeth.

"Would you rather I let you keep it and turn it over to the authorities and let you explain what the hell you were doing with it? This was not a game to be played out your way, Darcy. Lives were at risk. These men will kill anyone who gets in the way of what they consider a million-dollar business. I could not take a chance on your life. I had warned you about Felder, but you wouldn't listen."

She lifted her chin and glared at him. "I could have handled him."

Did she not hear a single thing he said? Was she *that* stubborn? At that moment, something inside him snapped. Did she think she was indestructible? A damn superwoman? Someone with nine lives or something?

She had the nerve to step closer, get in his face. "You used me."

He rolled his eyes. "If that's what you want to think, go right ahead. But when you calm down you'll realize what I did was keep you alive."

"I don't see it that way."

"One day you will."

And before she could utter another word, he captured her mouth with his, went at it with a hunger that even surprised him. He knew she was mad, and it would probably take a long time for her to get over things. He'd heard that she could hold a grudge like nobody's business. But he'd had to take his chances. At least she was alive and wasn't in any danger.

Her heart was beating just as fast and intense as his, and he released her mouth long enough to draw in air that was drenched with her scent — an indication that she wanted him as much as he wanted her. Their gazes connected. At that moment, heat surged between them, so strong it nearly singed his insides.

He was definitely undone.

Without any type of control, he reached out and his hands ripped the silk gown off her body. He tossed the shreds of torn fabric to the floor. He was about to take her like she'd probably never been taken before. She was in his blood, in his mind. And heaven help him, the woman had somehow wiggled her way into his heart. And she had the nerve to assume that he would let her walk blindly into a dangerous situation?

He opened his mouth to say something and couldn't. What could he say? An admission of love probably wouldn't ring true to her ears right now anyway. So he would speak in a way that they communicated so well, with their bodies. Whenever they were inside each other they were of one mind, like two peas in a pod. And Lord knew he needed to get all inside that luscious pod of hers.

Time passed that was measured by the beats of their hearts, a thrumming sound that enlarged his erection with every single tick of the clock. And then he growled, a primitive sound that rented the air, as he lowered his gaze to her naked body and saw everything he wanted, everything he needed, every single thing he loved and desired.

He unzipped his jeans and quickly stepped out of them, flung them aside. He reached out and drew her into his arms and hungrily captured her mouth once again and began mating with it in a frenzy that he felt down to his gut.

He felt the moment tension flowed from her shoulders, the moment she forgot all about her anger for the time being to concentrate on their kiss. It was just as fiery and passionate as all the others. He sank his fingers in her hair, felt her scalp and he deepened the kiss. It was as if he couldn't get enough of her, and the more he got, the more he wanted.

It seemed her hunger was just as intense as his was for her. She had taken him in her hand, was stroking his head and he felt his erection get larger beneath her fingers. She broke the kiss to breathe against his moist lips. "Hurry, York. I want you now!"

He heard the hunger in her voice. She might still be mad at him, but at the moment she would put her anger aside for this. So would he. There would be a lot to talk about later. And they would talk. Their future depended on an in-depth discussion and whether she wanted to accept it or believe it, they had a future. He now knew how it felt to love a woman to the point where you felt it in every bone in your body, and the need to become one with her was as vital as breathing.

She twisted out of his arms. "You're taking too long."

The moment her feet touched the floor she fell to her knees and took him into her mouth. And he let out a groan that nearly pierced the back of his throat. Immense heat surged in his testicles, and he felt them about to burst. He knew what she was doing. She wanted as much juice from him as his body could produce, and she was making sure there would be plenty by drawing out the lust in him.

If only she knew. There was no longer lust — only love.

When he felt his body almost explode in her mouth, he held back. And then without warning he dropped down on his knees and turned her around so that her back was pressed against his chest, her backside snug against his erection. And then his fingers felt around for her, felt the moist heat of her feminine mound, and like radar, the head of his erection found her and he eagerly thrust inside her.

"Hold on, baby. I'm going to ride you good," he whispered hotly, close to her ear, and she threw her head back and moaned with every single thrust into her body. He cradled her hips tight into the breadth of his thighs while he pounded into her and she begged for more.

He reached around her and let his fingers caress the tips of her breasts, cupped them in his hands and kneaded them to his heart's content. Her nipples were firm, erect, like pebbles in his hands. And he knew at that moment he would never, ever get enough of her and that Darcy Owens would be a permanent fixture in his life.

■ ■ ■ ■

Darcy felt York in every part of her body each time he pounded into her and then withdrew only to thrust back. He had her thighs spread wide, and she could feel the heat of his chest on hers. He was riding her in a way she'd never been ridden before, driving her insane with pleasure. And when she was to the point of detonating he would slowly ease out of her and in one hard thrust, find his way back in. Over and over again.

He was literally breaking her down with a need she only knew about since meeting him. She was desperate to have him, to feel him come inside of her, drench her with his release. Intense pleasure was thrumming, bursting to life in her feminine core, making her whimper, moan, and she knew soon he would have her screaming.

He thrust deeper inside of her, and she wondered how that was possible. It was as if his shaft had grown in length to accommodate her needs and desires. And then she felt her body buck into an explosion, detonate in rapture and she screamed. It seemed her scream torched something within him, and he rammed into her even deeper, just seconds before exploding.

"Yes! Yes! Yes!" She felt the essence of him spill into her, flood her in a thick, heated bath of release. It did something to her, and she sucked in a deep breath; with it came the scent of mingled bodies, tantalizing sex. This was pleasure beyond anything they had ever shared, and she knew that as much as she enjoyed it that this would be it for them. The end. He had deliberately kept her with him last night for a reason. It had nothing to do with wanting her but all to do with solving his case.

But she was convinced that now, at this moment, he needed her. And she hoped he realized that when she left and would refuse to see him again. This was more than a parting gift. This would fuel his thoughts of what he would never have again.

She pushed the thoughts out of her mind when he kept going for another round and her body was in full agreement when another orgasm swept through her the same time it did him. She gloried in the feel of his hardness exploding into her once again, and she knew at that moment that she loved him. She loved every part of him, but because of what he'd done, her love would not be enough to consider forgiving him.

■ ■ ■ ■

York wasn't sure what woke him up, but he opened his eyes and glanced at the clock on his nightstand. It was almost two in the afternoon. He closed his eyes wanting to remember every detail of what had happened between him and Darcy after breakfast. He smiled as he recalled every luscious detail of them making love — doggy style — on his kitchen floor, showering together afterward before falling into his bed and making love again.

He opened his eyes knowing the time had come for them to talk. He needed to explain why he could not have let her take part in exposing Felder. She meant too much to him, and there was no way he could have put her at any risk. He loved her.

His phone rang, and he quickly eased out of bed and glanced over his shoulder. The place where Darcy had lain was empty. He figured she had probably gotten hungry and had gone downstairs to grab something to eat. After all, it was way past lunchtime.

He grabbed for the phone and recognized the number. "Yes, Wesley?"

"Mission accomplished."

He smiled knowing what that meant.

Once again, his men had done an outstanding job. He had wanted to be there, right in the thick of things, but he had been needed here to keep his woman out of trouble, out of harm's way. "I need full details. Give me a minute to get downstairs to my office, and I'll call you right back."

He hung up the phone and glanced around and immediately knew something was wrong. Darcy's overnight bag, the one that had been sitting next to his dresser, was gone. He quickly went into the bathroom and found his vanity cleaned of her belongings. It was as if she'd never been there.

Grabbing a robe, like a madman he tore out of the room and rushed down the stairs. But the house was empty. He moved back to the kitchen and saw the note she had scribbled and left on the front of his refrigerator. She had written the message with red lipstick.

You got what you wanted. Now stay away from me!

Fuming, he snatched the paper off his refrigerator and crushed it in his hands before tossing it in a nearby trash can. He growled deep in his throat. "Like hell I will."

CHAPTER 14

"If you think finally getting around to admitting you had an affair with York in Jamaica will exonerate you from spending New Year's with me then you are wrong, Darcelle Owens."

Darcy rolled her eyes as she stood at the window in her New York house. It was two days after Christmas. If her parents had been surprised that she had shown up on their doorstep a few days earlier than planned, they didn't let on. And she knew her brothers had been itching to ask why her eyes were so swollen and her nose was red. Instead, they did what they usually did when she was a kid and would fly into the house crying from a boo-boo. They would cuddle her and try to kiss her hurt away.

And for a while she was able to get York Ellis out of her mind but not out of her heart. Instead of leaving her parents' home the day after Christmas as planned to head to Cavanaugh Lake, she had returned home to New York, determined to spend New Year's alone. She was not surprised that Ellie wasn't happy with that decision. Even after confessing and telling her friend everything, she wasn't budging.

"Did you hear everything I said, El?"

"Yes, I heard you. I saw York on Christmas Day in Phoenix when everyone flew in for Eli Steele's wedding. He didn't give anything away."

That meant out of sight, out of mind. She hadn't expected anything other than that anyway. She wouldn't be surprised if Ellie mentioned he had brought someone. She wouldn't ask for fear of finding out something she didn't want to know, something that would break her heart even more.

"Besides, Darcy," Ellie broke into her thoughts and said, "I heard on the news about that case his company busted. From what I understand it was pretty dangerous, so I'm glad he kept you from getting involved."

Darcy frowned. "I could have handled my own."

"Are you listening to me? Those men would not have hesitated to hurt you if you tried to disrupt their plan."

But still . . .

"He used me," she said, determined for her best friend to see her point. She needed some sympathy here.

"And I'm sure you used him as well, so get over it, Dar, and catch a plane here."

She nibbled on her bottom lip. "I'm not ready to see him, and chances are he'll be there."

"Yes, he will be. But that shouldn't stop you from coming as well. It will be business as usual since you and York have always avoided each other anyway." There was a pause, then Ellie said, "Unless there is more to it than what you're telling me."

Darcy continued nibbling on her lip. "More like what?"

"Your true feelings for him. You sound more like a woman in love than a woman upset for not getting her way."

Darcy frowned. "I'm not in love with York!" Maybe if she said it enough times she would be able to convince herself of that.

"Um, if you say so. Look, I need to get out of here and go to the grocery store, but I'll call you later. The weather around the lake is beautiful. You don't know what you're missing."

Darcy wiped a tear that had just fallen from her eye. "Yes, I do." *I won't be seeing*

York again anytime soon.

"Is there a message you want me to give York when I see him?" Ellie asked.

"Of course not. He means nothing to me. I just don't like being played."

"Well, it sounds to me you're getting played confused with protected. I'll talk to you later, Darcy."

She heard the phone click in her ear and shook her head. What did Ellie know? She loved a man who loved her back. Some women had all the luck. Not ready to start her day yet, she tightened her robe around her and headed toward the kitchen to grab something for breakfast.

Since she'd planned to be away for the holidays, she hadn't put up a tree this year. But she had decorated the fireplace with garland and had even hung out the stocking her secretary's eight-year-old daughter had made for her last Christmas.

With a cup of hot chocolate and small plate of crescent rolls, she went back to the living room to enjoy her breakfast alone. Turning on the television, she saw that more arrests had been made in the case York and his people had cracked, including members of the Medina family. She even caught a quick glimpse of a handcuffed Damien being led away by authorities. Feeling even

249

more depressed she turned off the television and finished her breakfast.

An hour or so later after cleaning up the kitchen, watering her plants and rearranging items in her cabinets, she decided she would take a nap. She might as well since she still had her nightgown on underneath her robe. She would treat this as a lazy day. She was headed toward her bedroom when her doorbell sounded. She figured it was her neighbor who'd been kind enough to collect her mail while she was gone.

Darcy glanced out the peephole and caught her breath. York!

Mixed emotions flooded her. On one hand, she was tempted to pinch herself to make sure what she was seeing was real. On the other hand, she wanted to open the door just to slam it in his face. It had been over a week since that morning when she had slipped out of bed to flee the island, needing to put as much distance between them as she possibly could.

Over a week.

And she hadn't heard from him. But she had to admit she had warned him to stay away from her. However, when did men like York do what they were told? And why was he here now? And why was a part of her glad that he was?

He rang the doorbell again, and she drew in a deep breath. "I can handle this," she muttered under her breath as she slowly removed the chain off the door. "And I can handle him," she added to assure herself as she slowly turned the knob.

The moment she flung the door wide and his gaze connected with his, she knew she'd assumed wrong. She couldn't handle him. He was standing there, leaning in her doorway. Her nose inhaled his cologne that mingled was the scent of primitive man. He was dressed in a pair of snug-fitting jeans and a blue pullover sweater, looking like the man he was, the man who'd captured her heart.

The man she loved.

"Darcy."

York studied the woman standing in front of him. Had it really been eight days since he'd seen her, eight days since he'd made love to her, heard her scream? Even with that little annoying frown forming around her mouth, she looked beautiful. She looked as if she'd raked her fingers instead of a comb through her hair. It was tossed in disarray around her shoulders, and the early morning sun gave it a sun-kissed luster.

"Why are you here, York?"

That question was simple enough. "I came for you."

She looked surprised. "For me?"

"Yes."

She crossed her arms over her chest, and the gesture uplifted her breasts. Her cleavage looked good, and he bet her nipples looked even better. His tongue seemed to thicken at the thought of being wrapped around one.

"Didn't you get my note? The one I left on your refrigerator?"

He shrugged. "Yes, I got it."

"And?"

"And I figured you were mad when you wrote it."

An angry tint suddenly appeared on her cheeks, and she just stared at him. York suspected that she was probably wondering what would be the best way to throttle him.

"Yes, I was mad when I wrote it and I'm still mad."

He held her gaze. "Then I suggest you get over it." And before she could pick up her mouth that had nearly dropped to the floor, he took the opportunity to walk past her into her house.

"Wait a minute. I didn't invite you in, York."

He glanced over his shoulder. "You didn't

have to."

She slammed the door with enough force to make the room shake. "Now, you listen here."

He turned around. "No, you listen here," he said back at her. "I've given you eight days, and I refuse to give you any more."

"Y-you g-gave me," she stuttered in anger.

"Yes. I would have come after you right away but I figured you needed to cool off and think things through. That gave me time to wrap up the case and attend Eli's wedding since I knew you'd already made plans to spend the holidays with your own family. But I talked to Uriel last night, and he mentioned you had changed your mind about coming to the lake."

"Not that it's any of your business, but I have," she said lifting her chin.

"Then you need to rethink that decision." He knew if she had something handy to throw at him, she would.

She crossed the room, and he could see flames bursting in her eyes. "Just who the hell do you think you are?"

He couldn't help the smile that touched his lips. "York Celtic Ellis," he said, moving to cover the distance separating them. "The last man you slept with. The only man you'll be sleeping with from here on out." When he came to a stop in front of her, he said in an even huskier voice, "I'm also the man who loves you more than life itself."

She nearly stumbled backward. "No."

He advanced forward. "Hell, yes. You might not ask for my love, probably don't even want it, but you got it, lock, stock and barrel."

"No."

"Why are you in denial, Darcy? There was no way in hell I would let you go into danger of any kind. Now I understand what true love is. I know what it truly is to love a woman."

Darcy stared at him, nearly frozen in shock at his words. She had to take a few moments to inhale and slowly exhale to fight the emotions that tried overtaking her. Did he know what he was saying? Did he understand the full impact?

She studied his features and saw the intensity in the dark eyes staring back at her. Yes, he knew and understood. She felt the sincerity of his gaze all the way to her bones when he lowered his voice to say, "I hadn't planned on loving any woman this much. I honestly didn't think that I could. You proved me wrong, Darcy."

His words propelled her to move, take a

step closer to him. "How wrong?"

"Very wrong. But in my heart I know I did the right thing keeping you out of that mess with Felder."

In her heart, she knew the same thing. She could finally admit that. Not only had he and the people who worked for him exposed the persons behind the black marketing of those movies but they were able to establish a strong connection between the death of York's former girlfriend and the Medinas.

For a moment she couldn't say anything. She just stood there and stared at him, and she knew Ellie had been right. Her stubbornness wouldn't let her see what was quite obvious. He hadn't played her but had protected her.

She inched a little closer to him and heard his sharp intake of breath when a hardened nipple protruding through her silk robe came into contact with his chest. Electric energy flared between them and sent a jolt to the juncture of her thighs. She could feel every beat of his heart. If her move surprised him, he didn't let on. Instead, he was watching her with those dark eyes as if waiting to see what she would do next.

Darcy didn't give him long to wait. She wrapped her arms around his neck and then leaned in closer to bring her lips just a breath away from his sensual mouth. "And I love you, too, York. So very much," she whispered.

By the way his brow arched, she could tell that he was surprised by that, and from the immediate curve of his lips she knew her admission had pleased him.

"But don't think for one minute that I'm a pushover," she warned.

"Such a thing never crossed my mind," he responded, wrapping his arms around her waist.

And then he leaned in to kiss her, and she didn't hesitate in kissing him back. The hunger was immediate, the desire apparent. She needed to be his woman, the one to whom he'd declared his love. She relayed it in her kiss with a relentless attack on his mouth. When he lifted her up into his arms and wrapped her legs around him, she knew it was just the beginning.

He broke off their kiss and stared at her. "Marry me."

She smiled. It wasn't a request. Instead, it sounded more like a demand. Would he never learn? "I'll think about it."

She let out a sharp gasp when he jousted her up and all but tossed her across his shoulders like a sack of potatoes. "York, put me down!"

"Soon enough."

It was a short walk from her kitchen to her living room, where he gently placed her down on the sofa and joined her. She couldn't help but laugh as she stared up into his love-filled eyes. And just to think she had fled New York three weeks ago because of the cold, and now she was back in the city surrounded by intense heat.

"There's nothing to think about, baby. I refuse to spend any more time without you, so plan a wedding."

She knew he was dead serious and deciding they needed to spend their time doing things other than arguing. She asked, "Would a Valentine's Day wedding be soon enough?"

"Yes, if I have to wait that long."

She smiled up at him as she reached up to entwine her arms around his neck. "I'll just have to make sure it's a pleasurable wait."

And then she pulled his mouth down to hers.

EPILOGUE

York smiled down at his beautiful bride thinking she had kept her word and it had been a pleasurable wait. But as of an hour ago, the waiting had come to an end. Darcelle Owens was now Darcelle Ellis and he couldn't be happier. However, a quick glance across the room at his remaining three single godbrothers showed they were just the opposite.

He inwardly smiled thinking sooner or later they would get over it. But then again, in a way he knew just how they felt. If anyone would have told him months ago he was headed for the altar he would not have believed them.

"Do you mind if I have a dance with my daughter-in-law?"

York chuckled as he glanced over at his father. His parents, like everyone else, had been shocked at his wedding announcement. "Sure, Dad. That will give me some time to go over and smooth three of your godsons' ruffled feathers."

His father laughed. "Good luck."

York placed a kiss on Darcy's lips. "I'll be back in a minute, sweetheart."

"I'll be waiting," she said, grinning up at him.

He couldn't help the smile that touched his lips. Darcy had been a beautiful bride and he would never forget how she'd looked walking down the aisle on her father's arm in her beautiful wedding gown. He was convinced the memory would remain in his heart forever.

York came to a stop in front of Winston, Zion and Virgil. He was glad to see all three of them, as well as Uriel and Xavier who were on the dance floor with their wives.

"So the traitor has decided to say a few words, has he?" Winston Coltrane asked in a clipped voice.

York nodded, smiling. He couldn't help it. He was definitely a happy man. "Don't hate, guys. Appreciate."

"Appreciate what?" Virgil asked, frowning. "The fact that another member of the Bachelors in Demand Club has defected? I see no reason to jump for joy at that. I hope you know what you've done."

York glanced over his shoulder at his wife

and couldn't help the way his gaze lingered on her a while as she danced with his father. He then turned back to his three godbrothers. "Yes, I know what I've done, and honestly, I don't expect the three of you to understand things yet. But I have a feeling you will one day. Trust me when I say I have no regrets in getting married."

"But you and Darcy never got along," Winston reminded him.

"Yes, but we definitely get along now," York replied.

"I guess you're out of the club," Zion said, shaking his head smiling. "And to think you were the president."

Yes, he'd been the president, and a staunch supporter of bachelorhood. "Sorry, guys, but I got a feeling one of you will be next. Probably in less than a year from now," York said grinning.

Virgil frowned. "Marriage has turned you into a fortune teller, Y?"

"No, just a happy man who wants to spread the cheer. I'll see you guys around . . . after my honeymoon."

Moments later he returned to Darcy and pulled her into his arms. She tilted her head back and glanced up at her husband. "They still don't look too happy with you."

He brushed a kiss across her lips. "I've

been where they are before. In fact, I'm the one who delivered the news to Uriel at his wedding that he was no longer in the club. Not that he cared."

York sighed and added, "Winston, Virgil and Zion see the club's members dwindling and can't help wondering what the hell is going on. That's three of us that have taken the plunge and three still remaining as bachelors."

She nodded. "What do you think they'll do?"

He tightened his arms around her waist. "Fight love like hell when it comes knocking on their doors. But in the end they will be what I had become."

"And what is that?"

"A bachelor undone by a gorgeous woman destined to be my soul-mate. You can't fight love. And I can't wait to see when they find that out."

Darcy glanced over at the three men, and thought she couldn't wait to see as well. That would definitely be interesting. She then glanced back at the man she had married just hours ago. York was her hero and the man who would always have her heart. Forever.

ABOUT THE AUTHOR

Brenda Jackson is a die "heart" romantic who married her childhood sweetheart and still proudly wears the "going steady" ring he gave her when she was fifteen. Because she's always believed in the power of love, Brenda's stories always have happy endings. In her real-life love story, Brenda and Gerald, her husband of thirty-nine years, live in Jacksonville, Florida, and have two sons.

A *New York Times* and *USA TODAY* bestselling author of more than eighty-five romance titles, Brenda is a retiree from a major insurance company and now divides her time between family, writing and traveling with Gerald. You may write to Brenda at P.O. Box 28267, Jacksonville, Florida 32226; email her at AuthorBrendaJackson @gmail.com or visit her website, www .brendajackson.net.